The Forbidden Dan

A Journey of Shadows, Secrets, and Self-Discovery

Camila Soriano

Copyright © 2024 by Camila Soriano

All rights reserved. No part of this book may be used or reproduced in any form whatsoever without written permission except in the case of brief quotations in critical articles or reviews.

First Edition: November 2024

Table of Contents

Chapter 1 Shadows in the Forest 1

Chapter 2 The Stranger's Flame 23

Chapter 3 An Unexpected Alliance 43

Chapter 4 Echoes of the Forest 65

Chapter 5 Reflections and Revelations 85

Chapter 6 Whispers of Doubt 106

Chapter 7 Mirror Lake 125

Chapter 8 Fighting the Flame 141

Chapter 9 Between Shadows and Light 156

Chapter 10 Divided Loyalties 170

Chapter 11 Visions of What Could Be 187

Chapter 12 A Choice Deferred 203

Chapter 13 At the Crossroads 218

Chapter 14 The Weight of Loyalty 233

Chapter 15 The Heart's Awakening 247

Epilogue A Path of Her Own 263

Chapter 1
Shadows in the Forest

The Forest of Reflections held its breath as Lyra slipped between the ancient trees, her movements so precise and controlled that she seemed like part of the forest itself. Every step was deliberate, each one careful to avoid the twisted roots that jutted from the misty ground. She scanned her surroundings in a practiced rhythm, her gaze flickering from the shadows on her left to the faint, silvery glows on her right. Nothing escaped her attention. The discipline drilled into her during years of training was evident in each movement, each calculated breath.

In the Eloryn clan, they called her *the Shadow*. The title wasn't a compliment or a mere nickname; it was a testament to her skill. She was a scout, the finest in the clan, able to blend with her surroundings to the point where even her own shadow barely followed her. Tonight, the forest was silent except for the soft rustle of leaves and the occasional murmur of the wind. But Lyra knew better than to let her guard down. The Forest of Reflections was deceptive. It had a way of pulling at the unwary, coaxing them into letting down their defenses.

Her hand hovered near her blade as she moved, her fingers brushing the hilt in reassurance. This forest held stories older than memory itself—tales of warriors who'd come face-to-face with reflections of their darkest fears or deepest desires. Some called it an illusion, others a glimpse into hidden truths. Whatever it was, Lyra wasn't here to satisfy curiosity. She was here to do her duty, to scout and report back. Duty was the only thing that mattered.

"Focus, Lyra," she whispered to herself, her voice barely a breath in the night.

Just then, a flicker of movement caught her eye—a shadow shifting in the mist to her left. Her instincts kicked in immediately. She stilled, sinking into a crouch, her body pressed close to the ground. Her senses sharpened, every muscle tensed, as she scanned the shadows. A wisp of fog curled lazily around the tree trunks, casting faint, ghostly shapes against the darkness. Her heart was steady, each beat measured and calm. Discipline wasn't just a practice; it was her way of life, the rhythm that kept her grounded.

The sound came again, faint but distinct—a rustle, barely audible. Her gaze zeroed in on the direction, eyes narrowing as she focused. There was no sign of life, yet her instincts warned her otherwise. She knew the forest could be treacherous, not just because of the creatures that lurked within, but because it had a way of distorting perception. Lyra had heard stories of warriors who'd seen things that weren't there, reflections of the past or visions of the future. Some claimed that the forest was alive, that it sensed the minds of those who wandered within it.

"Just shadows," she murmured, almost convincing herself. But she kept her stance ready, fingers resting lightly on her blade.

A chill crept through the air, not from the cold but from something else—an awareness, as if the forest itself was watching. Lyra steadied her breathing, reminding herself of her training. Her purpose here was simple: observe, assess, and report. Curiosity, she reminded herself, had no place in her mission.

But a voice—a barely-there whisper—drifted through her mind. *What if you're meant to see something more?*

She shook it off, gritting her teeth as she dismissed the errant thought. *Focus.* This forest may have been filled with mystery, but she wasn't here to uncover its secrets. She took another step forward, her gaze shifting from the mist-shrouded trees to the ground beneath her feet, careful to avoid making any unnecessary noise. Her ears strained, listening for the slightest indication of movement, her body tense but ready.

Suddenly, a low murmur reached her, so quiet it was almost a hum. It was neither animal nor wind. It was something else entirely—a soft, steady rhythm that seemed to pulse through the trees, almost like a heartbeat. She stiffened, her fingers instinctively tightening around the hilt of her weapon.

"Is someone there?" she whispered, her voice calm but firm.

Silence answered her, the forest resuming its eerie stillness. But she knew she hadn't imagined it. The faint hum lingered, threading through the silence like an uninvited guest. It felt… alive, as though the forest were breathing alongside her, observing her every move. Lyra forced herself to focus, pushing down the unsettling feeling that tried to creep into her thoughts.

Then, a flicker of light caught her attention—a subtle, silvery glow emanating from somewhere deeper within the trees. She narrowed her eyes, debating whether to investigate or remain on her course. Her orders were clear, yet the light held an inexplicable pull, as if it were calling her.

"No distractions," she reminded herself sharply. "Stay focused."

But the light didn't fade. If anything, it grew brighter, casting a soft glow through the mist. She took a deep breath, steadying herself. She had learned to resist impulses, to follow orders without question. But there was something in that light, something that stirred a curiosity she had long suppressed.

Finally, she took a step closer, moving toward the glow with careful precision. Her mind raced with questions she didn't allow herself to voice. Her focus never wavered, yet she couldn't shake the feeling that this light was different. It wasn't the ordinary reflection of moonlight on leaves or a trick of the mist. It was something… deliberate, almost like a beacon.

The closer she moved, the more defined the glow became, taking shape between the trees, as if guiding her. Lyra's disciplined mind fought against the lure, but the pull was undeniable. She would allow herself just a glimpse, she decided, only enough to understand if it posed a threat. Her mission was paramount, and anything that could compromise it had to be understood.

As she drew near, her eyes caught a glimpse of movement within the glow—a shadow that seemed to mirror her own. She halted, instincts on high alert. The shadow shifted and wavered, then stilled, hovering just at the edge of the light.

"Who are you?" she whispered, her voice steady despite the sudden tension that shot through her.

Silence greeted her once more, yet the shadow seemed to answer in its own way, reflecting her stance, her gaze. It was as though the forest were showing her something—something hidden, something that belonged to her. A strange chill trickled down her spine, but she held her ground, staring into the shadow that looked so much like herself yet felt foreign.

Her fingers hovered over her blade, her disciplined resolve clashing with a stirring sense of curiosity she couldn't fully suppress. The forest's silence deepened, wrapping around her like a cloak, and she felt, for the first time, the weight of its mysteries settling on her shoulders.

Then, as suddenly as it had come, the light faded, dissolving back into the mist, leaving her alone once more. The shadow vanished, the hum ceased, and the forest returned to its natural, unyielding stillness.

Lyra remained where she stood, her heartbeat steady yet somehow echoing with a strange resonance. Whatever that was, she couldn't let it distract her. With one final glance into the darkness, she turned, slipping back into the forest's depths, resuming her mission as though nothing had happened. But the memory of that shadow lingered, a ghostly reminder of something she couldn't name but couldn't ignore.

The forest was silent, save for the faint rustle of leaves shifting in the gentle night breeze. Lyra had barely resumed her scouting pace when a presence flickered in her periphery—a figure standing just beyond a tangle of silver-veined branches. Her hand instinctively went to the hilt of her weapon, muscles tensing as she narrowed her gaze on the intruder.

He was leaning casually against a tree, his posture loose, almost careless. He wore light armor, different from any she had seen before, with faint burnished edges that caught the sparse moonlight filtering through the mist. He looked almost... relaxed, as though he had been there all along, waiting.

"You know, you Eloryn have a certain reputation," he drawled, a faint smirk pulling at his lips. "Quiet, disciplined, invisible. And yet here you are, staring right at me. Not so invisible after all."

Lyra's grip tightened on her weapon. "You're in Eloryn territory," she replied, her voice cold, controlled. "You shouldn't be here."

He shrugged, his posture unchanging. "Shouldn't, maybe. But I am, aren't I?" He tilted his head, studying her with an amused glint in his eyes, which were a startlingly bright shade of amber. "I'm just passing through. No need to get all... intense."

"I am not intense." Lyra's words were clipped, irritation slipping through despite herself. She held his gaze, refusing to be disarmed by his casual demeanor.

"Could've fooled me," he replied, grinning openly now. "The name's Kian, by the way. And you are?"

"Leaving," she answered flatly, keeping her tone steely as she took a measured step back. But he didn't move, and something in his expression—the way he seemed completely at ease, as though her presence was neither a surprise nor a threat—made her pause.

"A bit harsh, isn't it?" He laughed softly, as if her hostility amused him. "I've heard the Eloryn are all about courtesy. Something about noble warriors and honor?" He leaned forward slightly, his eyes glinting with mischief. "Guess I was misinformed."

Her fingers tightened around her weapon, her posture rigid. "We have honor. But we also have boundaries—and you're crossing one."

"Oh, come on." He rolled his eyes, crossing his arms as if they were in the middle of a casual conversation instead of a tense standoff. "I'm not hurting anything, just... exploring." He gestured around him, as if to underscore the harmlessness of his presence. "The forest's too quiet tonight, don't you think? Makes you wonder what it's hiding."

Lyra's jaw clenched. His nonchalance was unnerving, grating against her trained instincts. In her experience, strangers—

especially wanderers from outside her clan—were rarely this relaxed, especially when caught trespassing. His confidence suggested he either didn't understand the danger or didn't care. Both possibilities troubled her.

"And why," she began slowly, not lowering her guard, "would a wanderer like you risk wandering into enemy territory?"

"Enemy territory?" He raised an eyebrow, clearly amused by her choice of words. "Strong term. I'd call it… undiscovered territory. Besides, what's life without a little risk?"

"Some of us prefer to stay alive," she shot back, her tone laced with impatience.

"And some of us prefer to live," he replied smoothly, shrugging as though the difference were insignificant. His gaze softened as he tilted his head. "So, which one are you? The type that stays alive, or the type that lives?"

"That's irrelevant," she snapped, irritation simmering beneath her calm exterior. "I'm here to keep my people safe, not to entertain wayward wanderers who think they're invincible."

"Oh, I'm far from invincible," he said, his grin widening as if her anger were a challenge. "But it seems to me you've got your guard up a bit too high. You ever stop to breathe?"

Lyra took another step back, tightening her stance. "And you ever stop to think?"

His laughter was soft, unhurried, as though he found her response charming rather than cutting. "Fair point. But thinking too much takes the fun out of things, don't you think?"

"No," she replied instantly, her voice edged with finality. "And if you have any sense, you'd leave now before this turns into something more… unfortunate."

"Unfortunate?" He chuckled, leaning back against the tree. "For who, exactly?"

"For you," she answered, her tone sharp, her stance unwavering. She was half expecting him to bristle, to show some sign of intimidation, but instead, he just looked at her, his gaze strangely curious.

"You know," he began thoughtfully, as though they were conversing over a campfire instead of locked in a silent standoff, "I didn't expect an Eloryn to be so… combative."

"We're not." Lyra's voice dropped to a cold edge. "We're protective. There's a difference."

"Protective." He echoed the word, tasting it like a rare wine. "Of what, exactly? Your territory? Your people?" His eyes gleamed with something she couldn't quite read. "Or just your peace and quiet?"

She ignored the question, tightening her grip on her blade. "Leave now, Kian."

"Or what?" He lifted his chin slightly, defiance flashing in his gaze. "You'll run me through right here, just for a little chat in the forest?"

Her gaze hardened, though her voice remained steady. "If I have to, yes."

He studied her, his expression turning almost serious for the first time. "You know, you're wasting a perfectly good moment to get to know someone interesting." He let the silence stretch, as if daring her to break it. When she didn't respond, he shrugged, a faint smile tugging at the corners of his mouth. "But hey, I get it. Rules and duty and all that."

Lyra's irritation flared again. He was trivializing everything she stood for, everything she'd worked for. "Duty isn't something to dismiss, wanderer," she said sharply. "It's what keeps us safe."

"And it's what keeps you…" He trailed off, as if searching for the right word. "Trapped."

The word hit her like a sudden blow, leaving a faint tremor of indignation beneath her otherwise steady demeanor. She drew herself up, meeting his gaze with a cold, steely glare. "I'm not trapped. I choose my path."

"Funny," he murmured, his voice soft, almost thoughtful. "Doesn't sound like much of a choice when you can't even spare a few minutes for a conversation."

She scoffed, crossing her arms. "I don't have time for pointless conversations with strangers who have no regard for boundaries."

"Maybe that's why you're so tense," he replied lightly, eyes glinting with mischief. "You Eloryn take life way too seriously. Sometimes, it's worth breaking the rules a little." He leaned forward, his voice dropping to a conspiratorial whisper. "You might even like it."

Lyra took a measured step back, her tone icy. "I don't need advice from a Kael wanderer who thinks the world revolves around his whims."

"Touché." Kian's smirk softened, a flicker of genuine curiosity replacing his teasing demeanor. "But you can't deny that you're just a little curious. Otherwise, you'd have sent me running by now."

She paused, realizing he was right. Something about his easy manner, his lack of fear, kept her from acting as quickly as she should have. But she masked her hesitation with a frosty glare. "Curiosity has no place here, Kian."

He raised his hands in mock surrender, a smile playing at his lips. "Then by all means, continue on your very serious, very dutiful path." He straightened, meeting her gaze with a steady intensity that held just a hint of challenge. "But if you ever feel like breaking the rules..." He let the words hang, his smirk widening. "You know where to find me."

Without another word, he turned and strode into the mist, his figure fading into the shadows with a confidence that grated against her disciplined instincts. Lyra watched him go, her thoughts tangled between irritation and a strange, unsettling intrigue.

Lyra barely had time to process Kian's exit before she heard his voice again, drifting through the mist like a playful echo.

"Thought you were leaving," he called, his voice carrying a lilt of amusement. "But here you are, still lurking. Didn't think I'd be so hard to shake off."

Lyra spun, irritation flashing in her eyes as she saw him leaning against a tree, arms crossed, that same infuriating smirk on his face. "I'm not lurking," she snapped. "I thought you understood that this territory is off-limits."

He laughed softly, shrugging as if the forest itself belonged to him. "You really believe that anyone outside your clan follows your rules? It's a big world, Eloryn. Your little forest here is just a small corner."

She scowled, stepping forward with a renewed firmness. "Maybe in your world, rules mean nothing. But here, we value order and respect."

"Respect?" He raised an eyebrow, feigning innocence. "I've been nothing but respectful. Haven't touched a single leaf. Haven't drawn a weapon. I'm just... admiring the view." His gaze swept over her pointedly, lingering just long enough to unsettle her.

"Save your flattery," Lyra retorted, though she felt an unwelcome warmth creeping up her neck. "I'm not here for games."

"Who said anything about games?" He held her gaze, his eyes glinting with mischief. "Maybe I'm just curious. You're the one acting like this is some kind of battle."

"It could be," she replied icily. "One wrong move, and I'll make sure you regret stepping foot into Eloryn land."

He smirked, tilting his head in mock contemplation. "Interesting. Is that what you're trained for, then? Fighting off curious wanderers? Or is there something more you're guarding?"

"I don't owe you an explanation," she said sharply, crossing her arms in a defensive stance. "Not that you'd understand."

"Oh, I understand more than you think," he replied, his tone softening, though the playful glint in his eye remained. "I understand that you're wound tighter than a spring and that all this talk of duty and order is just a way of keeping people at arm's length."

"You don't know anything about me," Lyra replied, her voice hard, though a flicker of doubt crept into her mind. "And I don't appreciate your assumptions."

"Assumptions?" He chuckled, his expression one of mock surprise. "Believe me, I don't need to assume anything. It's all there, written in that stern expression of yours." He paused, leaning in slightly, his tone dropping to a whisper. "Tell me, Lyra, do you ever let yourself relax? Or is this"—he gestured to her rigid stance—"all there is?"

Her jaw clenched, and she took a step back, though she refused to look away. "My purpose isn't to 'relax,' as you put it. I'm here to serve my clan, to keep them safe from intrusions like yours."

"Oh, so I'm an intrusion now?" He grinned, amusement dancing in his eyes. "Interesting choice of words. I'd say I'm more of an… unexpected guest."

"A guest wouldn't ignore clear boundaries," she shot back, folding her arms more tightly. "A guest would respect the rules of their host."

"And if I were to respect your rules?" he asked, leaning back with a casual shrug. "What then? You'd go back to wandering this forest in silence, never even stopping to think that there's more out there?"

"More out there?" she repeated, unable to hide her exasperation. "Is that how you justify aimless wandering? Telling yourself there's some grand mystery waiting for you?"

"Maybe I just know something you don't," he replied, his voice low, almost teasing. "Maybe there's a freedom in not being tied down by anyone else's rules."

She rolled her eyes, her patience wearing thin. "That's called irresponsibility, not freedom. Only a fool thinks he's free when he has no direction."

"Or maybe," he countered, taking a step closer, "it's the ones who cling to rules and walls that are the real prisoners."

His words hit closer than she wanted to admit, stirring an uninvited curiosity. "And what would you know about freedom, wanderer? You talk a lot, but all I see is someone who's lost."

"Lost?" He laughed, the sound soft and warm, laced with an undercurrent of something deeper. "No, not lost. I'm exactly where I need to be." He looked at her, his gaze steady, and she felt her breath hitch at the intensity in his eyes.

"What's that supposed to mean?" she demanded, unnerved by his gaze yet unwilling to look away.

He shrugged, his eyes still fixed on her. "Maybe you're asking the wrong questions."

Her brows knitted in frustration. "And what questions should I be asking?"

He leaned forward, his voice dropping to a near-whisper, his tone laced with challenge. "Why are you so afraid to even entertain the idea that there's more to life than duty? More than just… following orders?"

She held his gaze, feeling her defenses falter as something stirred within her. "I'm not afraid," she replied, though her voice lacked the conviction she intended. "I know my purpose."

"Your purpose," he echoed, his voice carrying a note of quiet mockery. "Is that all there is? Just… purpose?"

She bristled, defensive once more. "That purpose has kept me alive, has kept my people safe."

"Maybe," he conceded, his voice soft, almost understanding. "But has it ever made you… happy?"

She froze, caught off-guard by the question. Happiness wasn't a word she often allowed herself to consider, let alone pursue. Happiness was irrelevant when duty and discipline were at stake. But something in Kian's tone, in the way he looked at her with that easy, unaffected curiosity, made her question her own response.

"What I feel doesn't matter," she replied, forcing her tone back to its usual chill. "What matters is loyalty."

"Loyalty," he murmured, nodding as if weighing the word. "Loyalty to what, though? To a cause? To a set of rules?" His eyes softened as he held her gaze. "Or maybe… loyalty to yourself?"

She opened her mouth to respond, but no words came. His question lingered in the air between them, and for a brief, unsettling moment, she felt the walls she had carefully built around herself waver. But before she could regain her composure, he took a step back, giving her a long, considering look.

"You're interesting, Lyra," he said, his voice surprisingly gentle. "I wonder if you'll ever see it for yourself."

"See what?" she managed, her voice tight, defensive.

He smiled, a faint, almost wistful expression in his eyes. "That there's more to you than all this." He gestured to her with a small wave of his hand, as if encompassing the armor, the stance, the guard she kept firmly in place. "I just hope you don't keep yourself locked away long enough to miss it."

She felt her irritation flare, but before she could retaliate, he turned and disappeared back into the mist, his figure dissolving into the shadows as easily as he'd arrived.

She stood there, rooted to the spot, the echo of his words settling uncomfortably in her mind. His lighthearted taunts and unpredictable nature had unsettled her more than any threat she had ever faced, leaving her with questions she wasn't ready to confront. And yet, despite her irritation, she couldn't deny a faint spark of something else—something far more dangerous than curiosity.

Lyra watched as Kian disappeared into the mist, his easy, confident stride unbothered by her warning or her blade. His laughter seemed to linger in the air, an unwelcome melody that danced around her even after he was out of sight. She took a deep breath, trying to steady herself, to remind herself of her purpose. Yet, the forest felt different, as if it too had been stirred by his presence, his words echoing in her mind far louder than she cared to admit.

"Foolish," she muttered under her breath, turning on her heel. She resumed her path, forcing her steps to remain steady, precise. But his voice kept threading its way back into her thoughts.

"Why are you so afraid to entertain the idea that there's more to life than duty?"

The question had pricked something inside her, a soft spot she hadn't known existed, and she despised the way it lingered. She tried to brush it off, shaking her head as if to rid herself of his words entirely.

"It doesn't matter," she said to herself firmly. "He's just a wanderer with no sense of purpose. Just another stranger too foolish to understand the importance of loyalty."

Yet even as she spoke the words, they sounded hollow. There had been something in his eyes—a hint of understanding, perhaps, or something deeper that felt unnervingly familiar. She huffed in frustration, speaking aloud as though the sound of her own voice might drown out the nagging echoes of his.

"What could he possibly understand?" She scoffed, her voice barely louder than a whisper. "He doesn't know me. He doesn't know anything about duty, about—"

"Duty, duty, duty," a voice echoed, startling her. She spun around, but there was no one there. Only her own reflection in the dim light, fractured by the mist that wrapped around the trees. "Is it really all you care about?"

She tensed, recognizing that the voice was her own, a whisper in her mind that she hadn't let surface before. Her fingers tightened on the hilt of her weapon as if it could anchor her, provide a tangible reminder of what she was here for.

"This is ridiculous," she muttered to herself, resuming her patrol. "I'm letting one careless stranger cloud my mind."

But his face, that relaxed smile, and the casual ease in his gaze were hard to dismiss. She could still hear his words, playful yet oddly perceptive, lingering in her thoughts like an uninvited guest.

"You might even like it… breaking the rules a little."

Lyra shook her head sharply, forcing her steps to quicken, trying to walk away from the memory of his smirk, his voice. But every step seemed to bring her closer to it. She could almost hear him again, that light, mocking tone.

"What are you afraid of, Lyra?" he'd asked, his words slipping through her defenses like water through her fingers.

"I'm not afraid," she'd said, but even as she recalled her answer, she felt a faint flicker of doubt.

Kian's face flashed before her again, the way he'd looked at her with that mix of amusement and something else, something that had reached far past her carefully constructed walls. She gritted her teeth, reminding herself of her role, her loyalty, and her purpose.

"He's nothing more than a distraction," she told herself, her voice barely louder than the rustle of leaves in the dark. "A foolish wanderer with no sense of direction or duty."

But as she walked, her mind betrayed her, replaying the conversation over and over, each line taking on a weight she hadn't felt in the moment.

"Has it ever made you... happy?"

Happy. She frowned, her steps slowing. Happiness wasn't something she had ever considered. Not in the way he had said it, with that casual certainty. Happiness was a fleeting thing, unnecessary in a life devoted to discipline and loyalty. It wasn't that she'd chosen unhappiness—it was that she'd chosen purpose. That's what mattered, wasn't it?

Yet, his words tugged at her like a loose thread, unraveling parts of her she hadn't even known were there. What did he know about her anyway? He hadn't seen the long hours, the sacrifices, the way she'd fought to earn her place, to protect the people who mattered to her. He was just a wanderer with no ties, no obligations.

And yet...

She could almost hear him laughing again, as if he could see right through her defenses, as if he understood the thoughts she wasn't willing to confront.

"Why do you keep fighting?" he'd asked, his voice low, almost challenging.

"To protect what matters," she'd replied firmly, yet now the words felt almost rehearsed, like a line she'd been taught rather than something she truly believed.

She sighed, slowing her pace as the mist grew thicker around her, wrapping the forest in an ethereal glow. A shiver ran through her, not from the cold, but from something far more unsettling. His question lingered, curling around her mind, refusing to be dismissed.

Was duty all she cared about? She had trained for so long, honed every skill, every instinct to serve her clan. It was her pride, her purpose. But what was that purpose beyond protecting borders, enforcing boundaries? She pushed the thought away, tightening her jaw.

"I know who I am," she whispered firmly, her voice steady, if only for a moment. "I know my place."

But as she walked deeper into the forest, his words seemed to follow her, echoing through the silence, through the mist, through the soft, almost mocking rustle of the leaves.

"Or maybe… you're just afraid of what you might find if you stop."

She halted, feeling a strange ache bloom in her chest, a heaviness she couldn't quite shake. For a brief moment, she considered turning back, going after him, demanding answers to the questions he'd planted in her mind. But no, that was exactly what he wanted. He was trying to unsettle her, to make her question things that didn't need questioning.

"He's a distraction," she repeated under her breath, forcing her steps to quicken again, refusing to look back. "Just a wanderer who talks too much."

But as she moved forward, her focus drifting back to her path, the forest seemed to close in around her, quiet and observant. She couldn't escape the faint tug of curiosity that Kian had left in his wake, nor could she deny the way his words had slipped past her armor, leaving a tiny crack in its surface.

With each step, the silence grew heavier, as if the forest itself were listening, waiting.

Chapter 2
The Stranger's Flame

Lyra moved through the forest with purpose, her steps deliberate, her posture upright. The air was thick with the scent of moss and damp earth, the trees towering above her like silent sentinels. The Forest of Reflections had always been a place of mystery, a space where warriors had to stay vigilant and grounded, or risk losing themselves. This was especially true for her, a scout of the Eloryn clan, trained to embody precision, focus, and control. Yet, tonight, she felt an unfamiliar tug at her thoughts, an intrusion she hadn't expected.

She paused, exhaling slowly, centering herself in the quiet. *Stay focused*, she reminded herself, mentally reciting the tenets of her training. "Duty, purpose, loyalty," she murmured, feeling the familiar weight of each word settle her mind. She had come here for a reason—to observe, to guard, to ensure the safety of her people. The forest was no place for wandering thoughts or idle distractions.

Still, the image of Kian's smirk, his infuriatingly relaxed posture, his glinting eyes—bright and knowing—kept slipping into her mind. She brushed the thought aside quickly, taking a firmer grip on the hilt of her blade as if the action itself could anchor her back into focus.

He's nothing more than a careless wanderer, she told herself, silently reprimanding her own mind. *And he's not worth a second thought.*

But as she moved through the forest, the memory of his voice echoed in her thoughts, a persistent reminder that refused to be silenced.

"So serious, Eloryn," his voice seemed to whisper, half-mocking, half-curious. "Do you ever stop to breathe?"

She exhaled sharply, frustration threading through her composure. *Why was he still here?* She had dismissed him, walked away, yet his words clung to her, shadowing her every step. The mere thought of him, with that easy, nonchalant smile, made her blood simmer with an unfamiliar mixture of irritation and... something else. She couldn't name it, but it unsettled her, made her feel exposed in a way she'd never allowed herself to feel before.

To regain control, she recited a mantra in her mind, one ingrained through years of training: *Discipline is strength. Focus is clarity. Duty is purpose.*

The rhythm of her thoughts steadied her, her mind finding its center once more. But even as she moved forward, that center wavered, a thin crack forming in her mental armor. The memory of Kian's laughter, warm and untroubled, slipped back into her thoughts unbidden.

"Maybe you're just afraid of what you might find if you stop," he had said, his voice teasing, but with a strange sincerity underneath it.

She clenched her jaw, her fingers tightening around her weapon. It wasn't fear that drove her—it was loyalty, she reminded herself. Loyalty to her clan, to the duties that defined her. Yet, as her steps echoed softly in the quiet, the thought struck her: Had she truly chosen this path, or had it been chosen for her?

"Stop it, Lyra," she muttered to herself, shaking her head slightly as though to shake off the persistent whisper of his voice.

But the forest seemed to sense her inner turmoil, the trees leaning in closer, the mist thickening around her. The shadows seemed deeper tonight, their shapes shifting subtly, as if the forest itself were waiting for her to confront whatever it was she kept trying to bury. The silence pressed in, a heavy, expectant thing, and she could almost feel Kian's presence again, lingering just out of reach, a memory she couldn't shake.

"Duty, purpose, loyalty," she repeated under her breath, her voice steady, even as her heart gave a small, disquieting flutter.

What are you protecting? his voice seemed to ask, and though she knew it was just a memory, she could hear his question as clearly as if he were beside her.

"The people who matter," she answered aloud, more to herself than to any imagined presence. Her words felt solid, grounding her back in the present. The people of her clan depended on her; their safety was her responsibility. That was her purpose—everything else was irrelevant. And yet…

A small voice in the back of her mind questioned, *Is that truly all there is?*

Her steps faltered for just a moment, her gaze shifting to the faint beams of moonlight filtering through the trees. She imagined Kian, out there somewhere in the forest, probably walking without a care, exploring without purpose or direction. His life seemed so unrestrained, so unburdened. The idea felt almost foreign to her.

"Ridiculous," she murmured, the sharpness in her voice an attempt to sever the thought. She had no use for his carefree attitude, his lack of responsibility. She had worked tirelessly to become the scout she was, to embody the discipline and loyalty of the Eloryn. She didn't need or want the kind of freedom he had. And yet, it nagged at her, a tiny thread unraveling the certainty she held so tightly.

"Maybe there's a freedom in not being tied down by anyone else's rules," she remembered him saying, his words edged with that knowing smile.

Shaking her head, she forced her attention back to her surroundings. Her purpose was here, in these woods, in the protection of her people. What did it matter if he walked through the world with nothing tying him down? She didn't need to understand him, and she certainly didn't need his words lingering in her thoughts. His was a life of recklessness and risk, a path she had no interest in following.

Taking a steadying breath, she closed her eyes for a moment, letting the cool night air wash over her. She would find her focus again, ground herself in the duties she had chosen.

Whatever curiosity he had sparked was just that—a fleeting thought, a distraction she would soon forget.

When she opened her eyes, her resolve had returned, her grip on her purpose tightening. She would patrol the forest, complete her mission, and return to her people without another thought of the wandering stranger who had dared to question her.

But even as she moved forward, resuming her path through the quiet shadows of the forest, she couldn't quite shake the feeling that something had shifted. Something small, perhaps, but undeniably present, as though a door had opened, if only slightly. And just beyond it, a possibility she couldn't name beckoned, waiting patiently, quietly, in the depths of the forest.

The forest had settled back into its natural rhythm, the gentle sway of leaves, the faint whisper of the wind threading through the trees. Lyra moved forward with determined strides, her senses sharp, her focus back on the task at hand. She had almost convinced herself that her thoughts of Kian had been nothing more than a passing distraction—until she heard the soft crunch of footsteps behind her.

She spun around, her hand instinctively reaching for her blade, but froze when she saw him. Kian stood a few paces back, arms folded and leaning casually against a tree, his expression filled with amusement.

"Really?" he said, shaking his head with a faint, playful sigh. "So tense, Eloryn. I'd think you'd be a little less jumpy by now."

Lyra straightened, her face hardening at his tone. "I don't appreciate being followed," she replied coldly, resisting the urge to bristle at his familiar presence. "Especially by someone who has no business here."

"Followed?" He raised an eyebrow, his lips curling into a half-smile. "Who says I'm following you? Maybe I'm just admiring the scenery." His gaze drifted around theatrically before settling back on her, his grin widening. "And what a serious view it is."

Lyra's patience was already wearing thin. She narrowed her eyes, voice low and clipped. "If you're so determined to play at being carefree, I'd suggest you find a different forest. This one doesn't tolerate fools."

Kian chuckled, unfazed by her hostility. "Ah, but where's the fun in that? I like a bit of challenge now and then. Besides"—he pushed away from the tree, hands resting easily at his sides—"I'm not sure I'd call this foolish. Dangerous, maybe, but foolish?" He shrugged, his tone light, teasing. "Now that's debatable."

Lyra's fingers itched at her side, and she clenched them into a fist to steady herself. "If you knew half of what lurks in these woods, you'd rethink that assessment," she replied, her voice holding a warning edge. "The Forest of Reflections isn't just a place to wander aimlessly."

"Wandering aimlessly is exactly what makes it interesting," he countered, his eyes gleaming with mischief. "Maybe you'd understand if you stopped taking everything so... seriously."

She crossed her arms, leveling him with a stern look. "I take things seriously because there are lives at stake. My clan depends on me to be vigilant. To keep people like you from treating this place like a playground."

Kian laughed softly, leaning forward with a spark of curiosity. "People like me? Now, that sounds personal." His voice was light, but there was an undercurrent of genuine interest. "You've got a thing against people who don't follow the rules, don't you?"

"Rules exist for a reason," she replied firmly, her gaze unwavering. "They keep people safe. They ensure order."

"Or they keep people trapped," he murmured, almost as though he were talking to himself. "Order isn't everything, you know. Sometimes, it's okay to step outside the lines a little."

Lyra let out a short, humorless laugh, her tone dismissive. "Spoken like someone who's never had to protect anything worth losing."

His expression softened, and for a moment, the humor left his face, replaced by something deeper, a glimmer of understanding. "Maybe more than you think, Eloryn," he said quietly. But before she could fully register the change, the playful smile returned. "But let's not ruin a perfectly good conversation with serious topics, hmm?"

"Serious topics are the only ones worth having," she replied, her voice flat, the hint of exasperation breaking through her otherwise controlled tone. "Your attitude toward danger is reckless. A person who ignores threats is a liability."

Kian chuckled, crossing his arms. "A liability? Well, that's one I haven't heard before." He took a step closer, his voice lowering with mock solemnity. "And here I thought I was just good company."

"You're a distraction," she said pointedly, barely keeping the irritation from her voice. "One I'd rather not deal with."

"Oh, I'm well aware of how much you'd 'rather not deal with me,'" he replied, grinning. "But it seems you keep running into me anyway. Maybe the forest has other plans?"

"The forest doesn't have plans," she said, rolling her eyes. "It's a place of reflection, not… destiny."

He tilted his head, feigning deep contemplation. "Reflection, destiny… maybe they're not so different." He flashed her an infuriating smile. "Maybe it's trying to tell you something."

"Like what?" She raised an eyebrow, her voice dry with skepticism.

"Maybe that there's more to life than duty and discipline." He leaned forward, a hint of mischief in his gaze. "Maybe even a little room for fun, if you're willing to try it."

She scoffed, stepping back to put a bit of distance between them. "Fun isn't something I waste my time on, Kael."

His grin widened, and he took another step forward, closing the space she'd just created. "Your loss," he replied easily, his tone as light as ever. "But you're missing out."

"On what exactly?" she challenged, crossing her arms, defying his closeness.

He paused, his expression softening. "On the chance to let go for a moment. To see things differently. To realize there's more to the world than rules and boundaries."

Her jaw tightened, and she held his gaze, unflinching. "And what has this carefree attitude gotten you, Kian? Besides wandering through forbidden places without a thought to the consequences?"

"A lot more than you'd think," he replied, his tone softening just enough to catch her attention. "Perspective, maybe. Understanding."

"Understanding?" She almost laughed, but something in his expression held her back. "Of what?"

He shrugged, his gaze holding hers. "Of what people are like when they're not trying so hard to fit inside someone else's expectations." He paused, his voice lowering. "Or maybe just a glimpse of who they are when they let their guard down."

For a moment, a strange silence settled between them, heavy with words unsaid. Lyra felt her resolve waver, an unfamiliar warmth creeping in at the edges of her defenses. But she pushed it back, grounding herself in the discipline she knew so well.

"Well, I'm not interested in letting my guard down," she replied coolly, forcing her voice back to its usual steadiness. "Especially not around someone who disregards every rule I stand for."

He chuckled, stepping back with a mock bow. "Then I'll try not to offend your delicate sense of order too much, Eloryn."

"It's not about order, Kael," she said firmly, crossing her arms as she looked at him with barely concealed frustration. "It's about responsibility. Something you clearly know nothing about."

"Maybe not in the way you'd approve of," he admitted with a casual shrug. "But I know enough to respect that it matters to you." He watched her carefully, his expression softening once again. "Maybe it's what I like about you."

Lyra's expression hardened, though her voice was tinged with something she couldn't quite name. "Like about me?" she repeated, narrowing her eyes. "You don't know me."

"Maybe not," he conceded, but the smile he gave her was genuine, even a little disarming. "But I think I'd like to."

She opened her mouth to respond, but the words caught in her throat. Part of her wanted to dismiss him, to walk away and forget the entire conversation. But his gaze held a quiet intensity that made it hard to look away. And for a fleeting moment, she felt a glimmer of curiosity—an unfamiliar spark that both intrigued and unnerved her.

But she quickly shut it down, forcing her gaze back into its usual coldness. "You're wasting your time," she said simply, turning her back to him. "I'm not interested in… whatever it is you're trying to offer."

"Fair enough," he replied, unbothered, his voice still light. "But I'll be around if you change your mind."

Lyra didn't respond, focusing instead on the path ahead as she walked away, keeping her stride steady. Yet, as she left him behind, she couldn't shake the strange, lingering feeling that he'd left something behind with her—something she couldn't quite ignore.

They continued through the forest, the silence between them thick and charged. Lyra kept her eyes forward, her every movement disciplined, her senses keenly attuned to the forest around them. But the quiet didn't last long. Kian broke the silence first, his voice softer than before, lacking its usual teasing edge.

"Do you ever wonder," he began, almost as if talking to himself, "what it's like to be… free?"

Lyra glanced at him, a mixture of curiosity and suspicion in her gaze. "Free?" she repeated, the word unfamiliar on her tongue. "We all have duties, Kian. Responsibilities that keep us grounded, that give us purpose."

He let out a quiet laugh, though there was little humor in it. "You know, that's what they told me too. Duty. Loyalty. Purpose. All those words, repeated so many times that they almost started to feel like they meant something."

Lyra's brow furrowed, her curiosity reluctantly piqued. "Almost?" she questioned, trying to maintain her usual distance.

He shrugged, looking down at the ground as they walked, his hands resting loosely at his sides. "For a while, I thought they did. Thought I had a purpose, a place, something to hold onto." His voice dropped, barely louder than a whisper. "But then, one day, I realized it was just another kind of prison."

"A prison?" She couldn't mask the skepticism in her voice. "Is that what you think duty is? Some kind of trap?"

He didn't respond immediately, his gaze drifting to a beam of moonlight cutting through the mist ahead. "Sometimes, yeah. When you're told over and over again that you owe your life to a cause, to a purpose… eventually, it starts feeling like you're just living someone else's dream. Not your own."

Lyra struggled to understand, her mind rebelling against the idea. "So you walked away?" she asked, her tone edged with disapproval. "You abandoned your duties?"

"Abandoned?" He raised an eyebrow, giving her a rueful smile. "I suppose that's one way to see it. But from where I stood, it felt more like survival. Like I was finally waking up."

She scoffed, her tone turning icy. "And what, exactly, did you wake up to, Kian? A life with no direction, wandering aimlessly?"

"Maybe that's how you see it," he replied quietly, his gaze unwavering. "But for me, it's the only life that feels real." He paused, then added, almost to himself, "Freedom isn't aimless. It's just… unbound."

His words struck her in a place she hadn't realized was vulnerable. She'd always believed in her duty, her purpose, yet his quiet conviction unsettled her. She turned to him, her tone guarded. "So, freedom means what to you? Being unbound from responsibility?"

He shook his head, his expression softening. "No. Freedom isn't about shirking responsibility. It's about choosing what to be responsible for. Deciding for yourself what matters, and not letting anyone else decide it for you."

She crossed her arms, her gaze unyielding. "And what have you decided matters, Kian?"

He smiled faintly, but his eyes held a trace of sadness, a glimpse of something deeper. "Living for myself, I suppose. Making my own choices, even if they're flawed. Even if they lead me into places I shouldn't be." He glanced at her, his voice dropping lower. "Like this forest."

Her heart gave an involuntary flutter at the intensity in his gaze, but she quickly masked it with a cool expression. "So, your idea of freedom is selfishness," she remarked, her voice cutting. "No loyalty, no purpose beyond yourself."

He looked away, a faint, wry smile tugging at his lips. "Maybe. Or maybe it's just that I've learned loyalty doesn't mean giving yourself up entirely." His voice softened, his gaze distant. "Once upon a time, I would've done anything for the people I thought I belonged to. But there's a point where giving becomes losing, where loyalty becomes... surrender."

She blinked, caught off guard by his words. There was a rawness in his tone, a hint of pain that unsettled her. "You don't trust loyalty?" she asked, her voice gentler than she intended.

"I trust it," he replied, nodding slowly. "But I don't trust what people do with it. I don't trust the way they use it as a tool, a way to bind others to their will." He let out a small, bitter laugh. "People will promise you the world in exchange for your loyalty. But when it comes time for them to give something back... well, that's a different story."

Lyra felt a pang of something she couldn't quite name, a strange empathy stirring beneath her defenses. "It sounds like someone betrayed you."

"Maybe," he said, his voice quiet, almost reflective. "Or maybe I just saw things clearly for the first time. Saw that all those promises were just... words." He paused, his gaze drifting off into the mist. "Empty words from people who only wanted power."

She studied him, noting the way his usual levity had faded, replaced by a quiet vulnerability she hadn't expected. "So, you chose to live for yourself," she murmured, more to herself than to him.

He nodded, giving her a sad smile. "I chose to live in a way that felt… honest. Even if it meant losing everything else." He paused, meeting her gaze. "Freedom's the only thing no one can take from you. Once you taste it, there's no going back."

She remained silent, her gaze fixed on him, her mind caught in a swirl of conflicting thoughts. His perspective was so different from hers, yet she couldn't deny that it resonated in a way she didn't want to admit.

He seemed to sense her inner turmoil, and he gave a small, almost wistful smile. "I don't expect you to understand, Lyra. People like you… you're stronger than most. You believe in something bigger than yourself. And maybe that's exactly what you need."

She swallowed, feeling an unfamiliar warmth creep into her chest. "Maybe," she replied softly, though a part of her wondered if it was true. She had always known her purpose, her path. But now, hearing his story, his pain, she felt a hint of doubt.

They fell into silence again, walking side by side, each lost in their own thoughts. She felt a strange ache in her chest, a mixture of curiosity and something dangerously close to empathy. She wanted to brush it off, to focus on the path ahead, but his words lingered, unsettling and intriguing.

Finally, she spoke, her voice a whisper. "What if you're wrong, Kian? What if loyalty isn't a trap?"

He looked at her, his gaze piercing. "Then I hope you prove me wrong, Lyra." His voice was soft, almost hopeful. "But just remember… loyalty isn't supposed to cost you your soul."

His words settled heavily between them, a truth she hadn't dared to consider. They walked in silence, and she felt the shift, the beginning of something she couldn't name.

The night grew deeper as Lyra watched Kian disappear into the mist, his figure melting into the shadows with that same unburdened stride. His departure left a hollow sort of silence around her, the forest suddenly feeling both larger and emptier, as though he had left behind an echo that refused to fade. She stood motionless for a moment, her fingers flexing unconsciously at her sides, and let out a slow, controlled breath, willing herself back into the calm, disciplined state she knew so well.

Freedom. The word lingered in her mind, strange and unwelcome, stirring a part of her she wasn't used to examining. She wasn't certain what it meant to her, only that it felt foreign—like a dream spoken of in stories but never something real, never something she'd allowed herself to consider.

Freedom, as Kian described it, sounded reckless, a concept untethered from duty, from purpose. But as she replayed his words in her mind, she felt the unsettling tug of curiosity.

"Freedom's the only thing no one can take from you," he had said, his voice quiet, almost reverent. She could still see the vulnerability in his expression, a pain hidden beneath his usual confidence. It was the first time she had sensed anything genuine in him beyond his easy-going facade. His words had carried a weight, a kind of longing she hadn't expected, and that quiet vulnerability had slipped past her defenses in a way that felt dangerous.

A breeze swept through the trees, rustling the leaves in a soft, sighing murmur, and she closed her eyes, letting the cool air brush against her face. *Focus, Lyra,* she told herself firmly, pulling her thoughts back to her mission. *Remember your purpose.*

Yet, her purpose felt strangely... out of reach. Kian's words had carved an unexpected crack in the wall she had built around her thoughts, letting in questions she hadn't considered before. His doubts about loyalty, his dismissal of duty as a potential prison—all of it went against everything she believed, everything she had been raised to uphold. But it was unsettling how his words resonated, if only faintly, a quiet whisper that dared her to question.

"Loyalty isn't supposed to cost you your soul," he had said, and the statement had lingered, twisting its way into her mind with a quiet insistence.

She shook her head, attempting to dispel the thought. *My soul isn't for sale,* she reminded herself, yet the reassurance felt hollow. She'd never thought of loyalty as a transaction before, but the way Kian had spoken, it seemed like he'd once given everything to a cause only to lose himself in the process. She wondered, briefly, if she was capable of the same sacrifice—and if her loyalty was as unwavering as she had always believed.

Her eyes drifted to the trees surrounding her, each one standing like a silent witness to her thoughts. She knew these woods well; she had walked them countless times, trusted them to guard her secrets, her worries. But tonight, they felt different, as though the trees themselves were alive with quiet observation, a reminder of the things she kept buried.

Kian's words were just that—words, from a stranger with no sense of direction, a wanderer with too much confidence and too little discipline. Yet, they pricked at her, leaving an impression she hadn't expected. She tried to dismiss it, rationalizing that his perspective came from weakness, from his own inability to stay loyal. After all, what did he know of real responsibility? Of commitment that required sacrifice?

Nothing, she thought, forcing herself to believe it. But as she took a step forward, her gaze fixed firmly ahead, the ground felt uncertain beneath her feet.

She looked up at the night sky through the canopy of trees, the stars barely visible in the thin slivers of open sky. She had often thought of those stars as markers of constancy, their light a reminder of the unchanging path she followed. But tonight, the stars seemed distant, cold, as if they were as undecided as she felt.

Lyra let out a frustrated breath. *Enough,* she told herself, her voice stern, echoing the commands of her training. This was no time to get lost in thoughts, especially thoughts planted by a stranger with no understanding of who she was or why her loyalty mattered. She was here for a reason, and that reason hadn't changed. Her clan depended on her vigilance, on her strength. There was no room for doubt.

Drawing herself up, she straightened her shoulders, her expression hardening back into the disciplined mask she wore so well. Whatever words Kian had left lingering in her mind, they didn't belong there. They were distractions, planted to stir her, to weaken her resolve. She couldn't allow that, wouldn't allow that.

"This is my path," she whispered to the silent forest, as if reaffirming her commitment to herself and to the trees around her. "Not his."

The words felt resolute, steadying her, though she could feel the faint crack still there, a hairline fracture in her certainty. It was small, almost imperceptible, but she knew it was there, a reminder of the vulnerability she had glimpsed in herself.

She clenched her jaw, her hands steadying on the hilt of her blade as she resumed her patrol, her eyes scanning the forest with renewed focus. There were no more distractions, only duty. And that was enough.

With one final glance over her shoulder in the direction Kian had gone, she turned back to the path ahead, her steps firm, her mind refocusing on the task. Whatever crack Kian's words had left, she would seal it with discipline, with loyalty. She would walk her path, the only path she had ever known, and she would not look back.

But somewhere in the back of her mind, the quiet whisper of his voice lingered, and though she ignored it, she couldn't completely silence it.

Chapter 3
An Unexpected Alliance

The forest had grown quieter than usual, an unnatural stillness settling over the trees. Lyra moved with heightened caution, her instincts humming with tension. She could feel the weight of something close by, something dark and menacing. The air was thick with an uneasy chill, and every rustle of leaves, every faint shift of the shadows, set her on edge. She was not alone here.

Then, without warning, she caught sight of a figure slipping through the mist. She stilled, one hand reaching instinctively to the hilt of her blade. The figure moved with fluidity, his form blending into the shadows as if he were part of them, but there was no mistaking who it was.

"Kian," she muttered under her breath, equal parts annoyance and relief rippling through her. Before she could call out, he turned, his eyes meeting hers in the dim light. A smirk flickered across his face, but his expression quickly shifted as he glanced over her shoulder, his gaze sharpening.

"Lyra," he said quietly, taking a cautious step toward her. "I'd hold off on the greetings if I were you. We're not alone."

She tensed, her senses reaching out as she followed his line of sight. And then she saw it—a shadow creature lurking in the gloom, its dark form slithering through the underbrush, its eyes gleaming with a cold, unnatural light.

"Shadow spawn," she whispered, her tone laced with dread. She had encountered these creatures before, and each time, it felt like facing the embodiment of darkness itself. "They're drawn to power, to conflict. We must have stirred it."

Kian gave her a wry look. "Well, that's comforting." He slid his weapon from his belt, his stance shifting. "I suppose this isn't the moment to argue over territory, is it?"

Lyra hesitated, glancing at him, her jaw clenched. She hated the idea of needing his help, but the shadow creature was inching closer, its movements eerily silent, its gaze fixed on them both. She tightened her grip on her blade, steeling herself. "No, it's not. But don't think this means I trust you."

Kian smirked, his tone light despite the danger. "I wouldn't dream of it. Now, shall we?"

They moved as one, their bodies in sync despite their vastly different fighting styles. The shadow creature lunged, its dark form twisting toward them like a shadowed viper, and Lyra ducked, sweeping her blade up to deflect its lunge. The creature hissed, recoiling, but quickly turned its gaze to Kian, its eyes gleaming with a malevolent hunger.

Kian grinned, his movements deceptively relaxed as he twisted out of its reach, his blade flashing in the low light. "Fast little thing, isn't it?"

Lyra shot him a glare. "Focus, Kian. This isn't a game."

"Noted," he replied, his voice quieter, more serious. He sidestepped the creature's next strike, bringing his blade up in a swift arc that caught it across its side. A dark, wispy substance spilled from the wound, dissipating into the air like smoke.

The creature hissed, its form shimmering as if it were about to vanish, but Lyra knew better. "It's not done," she warned, her tone sharp. "They adapt quickly. We have to be faster."

Kian's eyes gleamed with excitement, his grin returning despite the danger. "Then let's give it something it can't adapt to."

He lunged forward, his movements wild but precise, striking at the creature's weak spots with an ease that surprised her. Lyra moved in tandem, her strikes calculated and controlled, aiming for the vulnerable points Kian exposed with his unpredictable approach. Together, they formed a rhythm, their contrasting styles blending into a seamless dance of steel and shadow.

"Nice moves, Eloryn," Kian murmured, ducking as the creature swiped at him with shadowed claws. "Didn't know you could keep up."

Lyra's expression remained serious, her focus unwavering. "If you stopped improvising, we might finish this faster."

"But where's the fun in that?" he replied, his grin widening as he dodged another strike, slashing at the creature's side. "Besides, you're holding your own."

"Because I have to," she shot back, her tone edged with exasperation. But beneath her irritation, there was a grudging respect for his skill. His style was unconventional, chaotic, yet somehow effective. Where she relied on discipline and precision, he wielded unpredictability like a weapon, throwing the creature off balance at every turn.

The shadow creature recoiled, sensing the shift in the battle, its form flickering as if considering retreat. But Lyra wasn't about to let it escape. She moved forward with a sudden burst of speed, her blade slicing through the creature's core in a swift, decisive strike. The creature let out a guttural hiss, its form unraveling into wisps of darkness that dissipated into the air.

They both stood still, breathing heavily as the last traces of the creature faded, the forest around them falling into silence once more. Lyra sheathed her weapon, giving Kian a cool, assessing look.

He returned her gaze, still catching his breath, but a smirk played on his lips. "Admit it. We make a good team."

Her expression remained impassive, though her voice held a trace of reluctant acknowledgment. "We were… effective."

"Effective?" He raised an eyebrow, grinning. "I'll take that as high praise from you."

"Don't get used to it," she replied, her tone sharpening as she straightened, brushing dirt from her armor. "This was a necessity, not a partnership."

Kian chuckled, clearly unfazed by her coolness. "Whatever you say, Eloryn. But I have to say, I'm impressed. You've got skills, and not just the stick-in-the-mud kind."

She narrowed her eyes, a faint scowl forming. "If you call me a 'stick in the mud' again, I'll show you skills you won't enjoy."

"Promises, promises." He grinned, his tone playful as he took a step back, his eyes gleaming with amusement. "But I'll take my leave, before you decide to 'impress' me any further."

She watched him, her expression softening only slightly, though her guard remained firmly in place. Despite his flippant attitude, there was a strange sense of camaraderie between them, an unspoken acknowledgment of their shared skill.

Before she could stop herself, she spoke, her tone quieter. "Thank you. For… helping."

Kian's smirk softened into something more genuine, his eyes warm as he held her gaze. "Anytime, Lyra. I'm full of surprises."

With a final wink, he turned and disappeared into the shadows, leaving her alone once again.

Lyra remained standing, her gaze fixed on the spot where he'd vanished. She hadn't wanted his help, hadn't wanted to admit that his unpredictable style had complemented her own. But now, as she stood in the quiet, she couldn't deny the strange satisfaction she felt from the battle, from the way they had fought together.

She took a deep breath, brushing the thought aside, reminding herself of her duty, her focus. She was here to protect, to patrol, not to entertain the notions of strangers who barely took anything seriously. Yet, as she resumed her path, she couldn't shake the faint feeling that something had shifted, that perhaps, working alongside Kian had stirred something deeper than she wanted to admit.

The shadow creature lunged forward again, its dark form twisting and contorting as it sought to overwhelm them. Lyra moved instinctively, raising her blade to block its attack, but the creature was faster than she anticipated. Just as she felt its claws graze her armor, a surge of flame erupted beside her, searing through the darkness and forcing the creature to retreat with a shriek.

She turned, her eyes narrowing as she took in Kian, who stood beside her, his hand extended, a small flame flickering at his fingertips. The light from the fire cast an otherworldly glow over his face, highlighting his intense focus as he prepared for the creature's next move.

"Since when do you use fire?" she asked, her voice edged with suspicion even as she steadied her stance.

"Since always," he replied, his gaze not leaving the creature. "It's just usually… less practical."

Without waiting for her response, he thrust his hand forward, the flame growing and arching toward the creature like a whip.

Lyra couldn't deny the effectiveness of the fire against the shadow spawn; the creature recoiled, its form flickering, uncertain in the face of the unexpected light and heat.

But as she watched, Lyra felt a strange pull—a connection forming between her own shadow powers and Kian's flame. Her shadows, which usually responded only to her will, began to shift, swirling and bending toward the heat, drawn like moths to a flame. It was as if her shadows were reaching out, harmonizing with his fire in a way that felt almost… alive.

She shivered, gripping her blade tightly, feeling her control waver. *Focus,* she told herself, but the sensation was unlike anything she had ever felt before. Her shadows pulsed in time with the rhythm of his flames, dark and light twisting together as they circled the creature, their combined powers creating a barrier that kept it at bay.

"Kian," she managed, her voice tense. "Your fire—it's pulling at my shadows."

He glanced at her, surprised, but there was a spark of intrigue in his eyes. "Interesting. I didn't know that could happen." His lips curved into a faint smile, though his focus remained on the battle. "Looks like they're not so different after all."

She shot him a glare, even as her shadows seemed to betray her, shifting toward his flames with a mind of their own. "I'm not here to experiment with 'synergy.' Focus on the creature."

"Oh, I'm focused," he replied, his tone lighter than the situation warranted. "But it seems our powers have other ideas."

The creature lunged again, its claws extended, and Lyra moved on instinct. She raised her hand, summoning her shadows to form a protective barrier, but instead of the usual controlled darkness, her shadows intertwined with Kian's flame, wrapping around his fire and magnifying it. The result was an intense burst of shadowy flames, crackling with an energy that radiated through the forest.

The creature let out a shriek, recoiling from the powerful blast, but Lyra barely noticed. She was too caught up in the strange sensation of her shadows mingling with his fire, the two energies merging and amplifying each other in a way that felt both thrilling and unsettling.

"Kian," she said, her voice barely a whisper, as if speaking too loudly might disrupt the delicate balance. "I can't control them. They're... they're drawn to your fire."

He looked at her, his gaze holding a glint of excitement. "Maybe they're reacting to the intensity," he suggested, his tone thoughtful, almost as if he were enjoying the discovery. "Or maybe they're drawn to each other—shadow and flame, opposites that complement."

"Complement?" she echoed, struggling to keep her voice steady as she tried to regain control over her shadows. "It feels more like they're taking over."

"Relax," he said softly, his tone uncharacteristically reassuring. "Let them work together. Don't fight it."

She shook her head, resisting the pull. "I'm not... I'm not used to letting go. My shadows—they respond to my will, my control."

"And maybe," he replied, his voice gentle yet firm, "they're stronger when they don't have to rely on just your will alone."

The creature roared, interrupting their exchange, and lunged forward once more. This time, Lyra didn't resist the strange pull between their powers. She raised her hand, focusing less on controlling her shadows and more on guiding them toward Kian's flames. The darkness and light twined together, forming a unified front that lashed out against the creature in a powerful wave.

The creature shrieked, its form dissolving as the combined force of shadow and flame overwhelmed it. Lyra watched, transfixed, as the last remnants of the shadow spawn dissipated, leaving the forest silent once more.

She lowered her hand slowly, the strange harmony between their powers fading, and turned to look at Kian. He was watching her with an expression she couldn't quite read, a mix of curiosity and something deeper, something almost... reverent.

"See?" he said quietly, breaking the silence. "Maybe your shadows don't have to be bound by control. Maybe they're meant to be free, just like my flame."

She bristled, the unease returning as she forced her shadows back into their usual disciplined form. "I don't want them free," she replied, her voice steady, though the experience had shaken her. "Control keeps them—and me—safe."

Kian sighed, a hint of disappointment in his gaze, though he masked it with a small smile. "Always so serious, Lyra." He paused, his gaze softening. "But just for a moment, didn't it feel… natural?"

"Natural?" She scoffed, though a part of her couldn't deny it. "It felt reckless. Dangerous."

"And yet," he replied, a faint spark of mischief returning to his eyes, "it worked."

She looked away, unwilling to acknowledge the truth of his words. The synergy between their powers had been undeniable, a force that neither of them could have achieved alone. But it was also unpredictable, wild—and that went against everything she valued.

"We don't need to do this again," she said firmly, focusing on the forest ahead. "This was a one-time necessity."

"Whatever you say, Eloryn," he replied, his tone light, though his eyes held a hint of amusement. "But you can't deny it. There's something between shadow and flame. Something that can't be forced, only… allowed."

She clenched her jaw, refusing to look at him. "I don't believe in letting anything happen without control."

"Maybe that's the difference between us," he replied softly. "I believe that sometimes, the strongest things can't be controlled."

Lyra remained silent, wrestling with the strange conflict his words stirred within her. The experience had left her shaken, questioning, and she couldn't afford that kind of vulnerability. She needed her control, her discipline—those were her strength. But as they stood in silence, with the remnants of their combined power still lingering in the air, she felt a faint, unwelcome sense of possibility that she couldn't quite banish.

With a final, steeling breath, she turned from him, resuming her path into the forest. But even as she moved forward, she couldn't shake the feeling that something had changed, that the harmony she'd felt with Kian's flame had opened a door she wasn't sure how to close.

The forest had settled back into an uneasy calm after the battle, the remnants of their combined powers lingering faintly in the air, like the ghost of an unspoken promise. Lyra kept her eyes on the path ahead, trying to refocus, to remind herself of the importance of solitude and discipline. But Kian's voice broke through her thoughts, lighthearted and entirely untroubled by the encounter they'd just survived.

"Well, I'd say that went rather well," he remarked with a grin, sliding his blade back into its sheath. "Shadow and flame—who knew we'd make such an impressive team?"

Lyra's jaw tightened, and she quickened her pace, ignoring the satisfaction his words sparked. "It was a necessity," she replied briskly, hoping the firmness in her tone would end the conversation. "Nothing more."

Kian chuckled, catching up to her with easy strides. "Oh, come on, Lyra. You can admit it. We handled that creature perfectly. I'd even say we were... complementary." His voice carried a hint of challenge, as though daring her to acknowledge their synergy.

She shot him a look, her expression impassive. "I'm not here to make alliances, Kian. And certainly not with someone who disregards structure and discipline at every turn."

His grin only widened, clearly enjoying her resistance. "You mean someone who doesn't follow all the rules," he corrected, his tone playful. "And yet, despite my reckless ways, you can't deny the result."

She huffed, folding her arms across her chest as they walked. "You were lucky. My shadows compensated for your lack of control."

He laughed, a warm, genuine sound that somehow eased the tension between them. "So that's what we're calling it—compensation? Seemed to me like you were keeping up just fine."

She bristled, a hint of irritation slipping through her disciplined exterior. "I don't need to keep up with anyone. I work alone because it's more efficient. Partnerships only create complications."

"Ah, but complications keep things interesting, don't they?" he replied smoothly, raising an eyebrow as he watched her with that familiar gleam of amusement. "Think about it, Lyra. Two fighters, two powers—different, but capable of creating something powerful together. Doesn't that even slightly intrigue you?"

Lyra hesitated, his words pricking at her carefully constructed beliefs. "I value efficiency, not… synergy," she said, though her voice lacked its usual conviction. "Your style is unpredictable. That's not something I can rely on."

"Unpredictable, maybe," he conceded, nodding. "But unpredictability has its advantages. We're not supposed to be carbon copies, Lyra. Different perspectives, different approaches—sometimes that's what makes things stronger."

She shook her head, her tone turning dismissive. "Unpredictability is a weakness. If I can't anticipate your moves, I can't trust you in battle. Discipline is what keeps people alive."

Kian tilted his head, studying her with a thoughtful gaze. "And yet, here we are, both alive, because we trusted each other enough to fight side by side. Admit it—our strengths filled each other's gaps."

Lyra's steps faltered slightly, though she quickly masked her hesitation. The undeniable truth of his words gnawed at her, unsettling her deeply held beliefs. "That was... circumstance," she replied, her voice quieter, almost to herself. "An anomaly."

"An anomaly?" He laughed, shaking his head. "If that's what you want to call it, sure. But it seems to me that you're just afraid to consider the possibility that your way might not be the only way."

Her gaze hardened, a flash of defensiveness slipping through her controlled expression. "I'm not afraid," she insisted, the words sharper than she intended. "I just know what works. Discipline, structure—those are the things that keep a person strong."

He looked at her for a long moment, his expression softening. "Strength isn't always about rigidity, Lyra. Sometimes, it's about adaptability. About allowing yourself to learn from others, even if it challenges what you know."

She opened her mouth to respond, but the words caught in her throat. She wasn't used to having her beliefs questioned, especially by someone who operated with such blatant disregard for everything she valued. And yet, the way he spoke—genuine, almost vulnerable—left her feeling disarmed.

"Do you always have to question everything?" she asked finally, trying to regain her usual composure.

"Only when I see something worth questioning," he replied, his tone soft, almost gentle. "And you, Lyra, are fascinating in that way. You're so certain, so committed to your path... but don't you ever wonder if there might be more?"

"More?" she echoed, struggling to keep the confusion from her voice. "More than what? Purpose, duty, loyalty? Those are the things that define me."

"Maybe," he agreed, nodding slowly. "But are they the only things? You're strong, yes. Disciplined. But there's a whole world of possibilities outside of that structure. Don't you want to see it?"

She looked away, her gaze fixed firmly on the trees ahead. "I don't have time for possibilities, Kian. I have a duty. That's all that matters."

He sighed, a trace of disappointment flickering across his face. "You're more than your duty, Lyra. I wish you'd see that."

She clenched her fists, unwilling to let his words penetrate the shield she'd built around herself. "I am exactly what I need to be. Discipline is the only thing that keeps people like me from losing control."

"Control," he repeated softly, as though testing the weight of the word. "But what if there's strength in letting go? In trusting someone else enough to share that control?"

She frowned, a mix of frustration and uncertainty simmering within her. "Trusting someone else is a luxury I can't afford. Not out here, not with lives at stake."

Kian watched her, his gaze searching, as though he were trying to see past her defenses. "Maybe you're right," he said finally, his voice carrying a hint of sadness. "But it seems to me that keeping everyone at a distance will only make you lonelier."

She felt her pulse quicken, a faint crack forming in her resolve. But she pushed it away, her voice hardening. "I don't need anyone's company. Least of all yours."

He laughed softly, the sound devoid of his usual humor. "If that's what you believe, then I won't argue. But just know… it doesn't have to be this way. You don't always have to do it alone."

She stiffened, unwilling to let his words linger. "Enough, Kian. I don't need your philosophy."

He held up his hands in mock surrender, though his eyes remained serious. "Understood, Eloryn. But remember—you can push people away all you like, but sometimes, working with others brings out strengths you didn't know you had."

She turned away, her heart thudding with a mixture of anger and something else she couldn't name. "Goodbye, Kian," she said firmly, hoping he wouldn't hear the slight tremor in her voice.

He watched her for a moment longer, then nodded, stepping back. "As you wish, Lyra. But I'm just a shadow away if you ever change your mind."

With that, he slipped into the darkness, his footsteps light, barely disturbing the silence of the forest. Lyra took a steadying breath, willing herself back into focus, back to the clarity that had always been her anchor. But his words clung to her thoughts, casting doubts over beliefs she had held for as long as she could remember.

She shook her head, forcing herself forward, determined to brush off his words as nothing more than the musings of a wanderer. Yet, a small part of her—a part she rarely acknowledged—couldn't help but wonder if he was right.

The forest was quiet once more, the shadow creature defeated, its dark essence dissipated into the mist. Only the faint echo of the battle lingered, mingling with the cool night air and the rustling of leaves high above. Lyra stood motionless, her senses still sharp, alert for any sign of lingering threats. But the forest seemed at peace, as if acknowledging the end of the skirmish.

She looked over to where Kian stood, his stance relaxed yet ready, his expression light despite the exertion of the fight. He caught her gaze, a slight smile playing at the corners of his mouth, and raised an eyebrow in that infuriatingly confident way of his.

"Well," he said, his tone both casual and expectant, "that was something, wasn't it?"

Lyra took a steadying breath, swallowing the words she truly wanted to say. Gratitude wasn't something that came easily, especially to someone as undisciplined and unpredictable as Kian. But despite her reservations, she knew he'd saved her more than once during their fight with the creature. She could feel the words forming, resisting the urge to dismiss him and walk away.

"Thank you," she said finally, her voice low and controlled, her gaze fixed somewhere over his shoulder.

Kian's eyes widened briefly, a glimmer of surprise breaking through his usual nonchalant demeanor. He tilted his head, as if savoring the rare moment. "Did I just hear that correctly? The ever-serious Lyra, thanking a reckless wanderer like me?"

She rolled her eyes, a hint of irritation slipping through her mask. "Don't make me regret it, Kian. I'm capable of gratitude, even if it's… not something I often express."

He chuckled, the sound warm and surprisingly genuine. "Well, I'll take it. Even if you look like you'd rather be anywhere else right now."

She sighed, shifting her weight as she fought to keep her expression neutral. "I just don't like owing anyone," she admitted, glancing at him briefly. "Especially not someone who treats everything as if it were a game."

Kian's smile softened, and he shrugged, the teasing edge leaving his voice. "For the record, I don't think everything's a game. Some things are… important. They just don't need to be taken with a grim determination." He paused, his gaze drifting toward the shadows around them. "Life's short, Lyra. There's value in taking things lightly sometimes."

She looked away, trying to ignore the strange pull in his words, that subtle challenge to her perspective. "Maybe for you. But my life doesn't work that way. I can't afford to be 'light.' Not when there are things worth protecting."

He nodded, studying her with that thoughtful gaze she was beginning to recognize, one that seemed to see through her defenses. "I understand that. But maybe one day, you'll see that strength doesn't always mean carrying everything alone."

The statement hung in the air, weighty and unwelcome. She clenched her fists, refusing to let his words take root. "I don't need anyone to carry anything for me," she replied firmly. "I have my own path to follow."

He sighed, a hint of resignation slipping into his expression. "I know. But sometimes, a little trust in others can make even the hardest path easier to walk."

She fell silent, unwilling to engage further, unwilling to give him the satisfaction of knowing he'd struck a nerve. Instead, she lifted her chin, staring into the mist that curled around the trees, as if to ground herself in the cool silence of the forest. She was here for a reason, with a purpose and a mission. She didn't need distractions, especially ones that made her question herself.

"Well," Kian said finally, his tone lighter, a faint smile returning to his lips, "I'll let you get back to your very serious, very solitary mission."

He took a step back, preparing to vanish into the mist, his movements as fluid and quiet as if he were part of the forest itself. But he paused, glancing over his shoulder at her one last time.

"Take care, Lyra," he said softly, his voice almost tender, the sincerity of the words catching her off guard. "Until we cross paths again."

Before she could respond, he slipped into the shadows, his form disappearing as the mist swallowed him whole. She stood there, staring after him, her chest tightening with an emotion she couldn't quite identify. She didn't want to admit it, but something about his departure felt… unsettling. As if a part of her hadn't wanted him to go.

She shook her head, willing the thoughts away. This was precisely what she couldn't afford—doubt, distraction. Yet as she resumed her path, she couldn't help but replay their conversation, his words looping in her mind.

"Life's short… there's value in taking things lightly."

It was a sentiment that felt foreign to her, even dangerous. She had been taught that strength came from control, that dedication meant discipline and focus, never allowing yourself to falter. And yet, there was a part of her, a small, quiet part, that wondered if Kian had found something worth considering—a way of living that didn't require her to hold so tightly to everything.

But that was a path she couldn't follow, a way of life that she would never allow to interfere with her purpose. She tightened her grip on her weapon, her mind settling back into the familiar rhythms of focus and duty. This was what she knew, what she had chosen.

And yet…

Even as she walked, her thoughts kept straying back to him, to the strange synergy they had shared, to the way his fire had harmonized with her shadows. She tried to dismiss it, to tell herself it was nothing more than an anomaly, a necessity brought about by circumstance. But deep down, she knew that it had felt different—like a force she couldn't control, something wild and alive that defied her usual precision.

The forest grew darker around her as the mist thickened, a shroud that seemed to mirror her inner conflict. She moved forward, each step deliberate, as if she could walk away from the questions Kian had left behind. But his words lingered, drifting in her mind like the mist that clung to the trees, whispering of possibilities she wasn't ready to confront.

Finally, she forced herself to speak, her voice a barely audible murmur in the night. "Stay focused, Lyra. This is what you've trained for. Nothing else matters."

The words were meant to ground her, to anchor her back to the unyielding foundation of discipline she had built. But even as she spoke, the conviction felt weaker than before, the certainty slipping just slightly. Kian's presence, his perspective, had left a mark—one she wasn't sure she could ignore.

With a final, determined breath, she pushed forward, her gaze fixed on the path ahead. She was a warrior, bound to her duty, and nothing—no distraction, no stranger's words—would change that. But as she disappeared into the shadows of the forest, her thoughts betrayed her, drifting back to Kian, to his easy smile, to the unsettling question of what it meant to live freely.

And though she tried to silence it, a quiet voice whispered in her mind, wondering if perhaps, one day, she might find out.

Chapter 4
Echoes of the Forest

The forest was shrouded in a heavy, whispering silence as Lyra made her way along the narrow path. The air felt thicker here, the mist curling around the trees, winding through the underbrush as though it had a life of its own. Every sound was muted, yet there was an undercurrent of movement—a faint shifting, as if the forest itself was watching, listening.

Lyra kept her gaze steady, her expression unreadable, moving with her usual precise steps. Yet, despite her training and discipline, she couldn't ignore the odd feeling prickling at her senses. It was as if the forest was aware of her, as if it were leaning in closer, waiting for something.

She shook her head, brushing off the sensation. "Just the usual forest magic," she muttered under her breath, though the words felt hollow. The Forest of Reflections had always had an eerie quality, one that could unsettle even the most seasoned scout. But this… this felt different. Personal.

As she moved forward, the mist thickened, twisting around her ankles like tendrils. Suddenly, a faint voice drifted through the silence—a soft, indistinct murmur, echoing in the distance. She froze, her hand going to the hilt of her blade, her heart steady but her senses alert.

The voice seemed to come from everywhere and nowhere all at once, a gentle hum threading through the trees. It was faint, almost like a whisper brushing against her ear.

"Lyra…"

She tensed, recognizing her own name. She scanned her surroundings, her gaze sharp. "Who's there?" she demanded, her voice low but firm, slicing through the silence.

Only the faint echo of her own words returned to her, as though the forest itself were mocking her. She waited, listening, but the only response was the soft rustling of leaves, the slight shiver of branches overhead. Her grip on her blade tightened, though she forced herself to keep her breathing calm.

"This forest is nothing but tricks," she murmured, steadying herself. "Old magic and echoes. Nothing to worry about."

But as she continued, the strange phenomena grew more intense. Shadows shifted around her, stretching and bending, their forms twisting into strange, indistinct shapes. The mist thickened, swirling like a veil around her, and she could almost swear that the shadows were reaching out, leaning toward her as if drawn by her presence.

She swallowed, fighting the unease that crept into her chest. "It's just the forest," she told herself, her voice firmer this time. "Nothing I haven't seen before."

But the shadows didn't relent. They shifted, coalescing into familiar shapes that sent a chill down her spine. She watched as the mist took on vague forms—shapes that resembled people she knew. Her fellow scouts. Her clan members. Her own reflection, staring back at her from the mist with eyes that seemed… empty.

"Lyra…" the voice came again, closer this time, soft and almost taunting. It sounded like her own voice, but twisted, distorted, as though it were coming from a memory she couldn't quite place.

She clenched her jaw, willing herself to remain still, unmoved. "You're nothing more than echoes," she said aloud, hoping her voice would shatter whatever illusion was forming around her. "Tricks of the forest."

Yet the shadows didn't fade. Instead, they seemed to grow, looming larger, pressing in around her as if trying to break through her stoic exterior. She could feel them probing at her, as though testing her resilience, searching for cracks in her control. The faces in the mist shifted, morphing, their eyes empty and hollow, yet somehow filled with accusation.

"What do you want?" she demanded, her tone edged with irritation, masking the faint tremor that threatened to betray her. "Show yourself, or leave me be."

The mist swirled in response, and for a moment, a figure seemed to form in front of her—a tall, shadowy shape, its features blurred, undefined. It looked almost like a person, yet it held no real substance. Its form flickered, bending in and out of the mist, as if struggling to hold shape.

"Lyra…" the voice echoed again, faint and haunting, but this time, it sounded softer, almost mournful. The figure tilted its head, and she felt an inexplicable pang of sadness, a sensation she couldn't place.

Her fingers tightened around her blade, her eyes narrowing as she held the figure's gaze. "Enough of these games," she said, her voice hard. "If you're some spirit of this forest, then make your intentions clear. I have no time for tricks."

The figure didn't respond, but the mist seemed to pulse, shifting in time with her heartbeat, as though the forest itself were breathing, responding to her presence. She felt a strange sensation, an echo of emotions she couldn't quite identify—sadness, regret, something deeper, something that felt… personal.

The shadows around her shifted again, the shapes becoming clearer, and she caught sight of faces from her past—memories she thought she had buried. She saw her mentors, her fellow warriors, their faces stern and watchful, their eyes reflecting disappointment, even accusation.

"Duty…" the voice whispered, drifting through the silence like a ghost. "Purpose…"

Her chest tightened, the words tugging at something inside her. She forced herself to remain stoic, to dismiss the strange pull of emotions that rose within her. "You're just shadows," she repeated firmly. "Reflections of nothing."

Yet even as she spoke, the doubt began to creep in, her disciplined exterior wavering just slightly. She could feel the weight of those words pressing against her, a silent question woven into the mist.

"What if this is all you are?" the voice murmured, softer this time, almost like a thought slipping through her mind. "What if there's nothing else?"

She clenched her fists, ignoring the way her heart pounded in her chest. "I know who I am. I don't need this… this nonsense to define me."

But the shadows persisted, the faces watching her with silent judgment. She could feel them pressing closer, as if waiting for her to acknowledge something she refused to see.

"Discipline is strength," she whispered, almost as if trying to convince herself. "I don't need anything else. I don't want anything else."

The mist swirled, the shadows shifting as the forest seemed to respond to her words. For a moment, it felt as though it were listening, waiting. Then, slowly, the faces faded, dissolving back into the mist, leaving her alone once more.

Lyra stood still, her heart pounding, her breath shallow as she scanned the empty forest around her. She shook her head, forcing herself to dismiss the lingering sensation, the strange crack in her composure.

"Just shadows," she muttered, her voice barely audible. "Nothing more."

Yet as she resumed her path, the forest's silence felt heavier, weighted with the echoes of things left unsaid, the subtle shift in her heart that refused to be dismissed.

The mist thickened around Lyra as she continued through the forest, her senses heightened, every shift of light and shadow drawing her attention. She couldn't shake the lingering chill from the strange encounter with the forest's illusions, her mind clouded by fragments of images she didn't understand. But she forced herself to focus, keeping her movements controlled, each step measured. She had to be vigilant here; the forest was alive, responsive to even the smallest flicker of uncertainty.

And then she heard it—a soft, almost mocking chuckle echoing through the trees. She halted, her hand instinctively moving to the hilt of her blade.

"Easy there, shadow warrior," came Kian's voice from somewhere to her left. He stepped out from behind a tree, his grin unmistakable even in the dim light. "Didn't mean to startle you. Though I have to say, you look a little… on edge."

She narrowed her eyes, her tone clipped. "I'm not on edge. I'm cautious. There's a difference."

"Cautious?" He arched an eyebrow, leaning against a nearby tree with that casual air that seemed to surround him like a cloak. "Looks more like you're ready to jump at every shadow." He gave a dramatic shiver, his eyes dancing with amusement. "What's got you so spooked, Lyra? Is the big, scary forest finally getting to you?"

She felt a flicker of irritation but forced it down, determined not to give him the satisfaction. "This forest isn't like others," she replied tersely. "It has a mind of its own, and it's drawn to those who don't respect it."

He chuckled, seemingly unfazed by her warning. "And what exactly am I doing that's so disrespectful? Enjoying the view? Wandering at my own pace?" He shrugged, a faint smirk tugging at the corner of his mouth. "I think the forest and I are getting along just fine."

Lyra scoffed, rolling her eyes. "It's not a matter of 'getting along.' This place has rules, and ignoring them is reckless."

"Reckless," he repeated, pretending to ponder the word as he took a step closer. "Isn't that just another word for… interesting?"

"Kian," she warned, crossing her arms. "You should be more careful. The forest isn't just a passive backdrop; it responds to… emotions. Intentions."

"Emotions and intentions, huh?" His eyes gleamed with a mixture of curiosity and amusement. "So, if I'm feeling particularly… mischievous, what does that mean for the forest?"

Before she could respond, a strange sensation rippled through the air. The mist around them thickened, swirling, as if drawn to the tension between them. Lyra felt the shadows near her feet darken, stretching out toward him, and she looked down, frowning as the darkness grew, responding to something she hadn't consciously summoned.

Kian noticed it too, his smile fading slightly. "Your shadows… they're reacting."

"So is your flame," she replied, nodding to the faint glow that had begun to emanate from his hands. His usual flame, a small and controlled flicker, was now brightening, casting a warm light that seemed to pulse in time with his heartbeat.

He held up his hands, inspecting the glow with a look of mild surprise. "Well, would you look at that? It's like the forest is… amplifying everything." He looked at her, his gaze sharper now, a spark of intrigue in his eyes. "Or maybe it's responding to us."

Lyra swallowed, feeling the weight of his words settle around her. Her shadows continued to deepen, stretching outward, blending with the mist, her power seeming to magnify of its own accord. She forced herself to stay calm, to contain the surge of energy building within her.

"It's… unusual," she admitted, her voice softer, almost as if speaking too loudly might disrupt the balance around them. "I've never felt the forest react this way."

Kian's expression softened, his tone quieter as he watched her. "Maybe it's sensing what we're holding back."

She shot him a wary look. "I'm not holding anything back."

He laughed softly, his eyes bright. "Sure, you're not. But the forest doesn't lie, Lyra. I'd say it's picking up on something."

She clenched her jaw, unwilling to entertain the notion. "You're imagining things. This is just… forest magic. Nothing more."

But even as she spoke, the forest seemed to disagree. The mist swirled closer, thickening around them, and she felt a strange pull, as if her shadows were reaching out toward his flame, drawn to it in a way that felt both natural and unsettling.

"Kian, control your flame," she said, trying to keep her tone steady. "If it gets any stronger, it'll overpower everything around us."

He looked at her, a flicker of challenge in his gaze. "And what if that's the point? What if we're supposed to let it grow, to let go of control?"

She shook her head, instinctively resisting. "Letting go is how mistakes happen. You should know that by now."

"Maybe," he said, his voice softer, his gaze steady. "Or maybe letting go is the only way to see what's truly possible."

His words stirred something within her, an unwelcome doubt that rippled through her mind. She took a step back, feeling the shadows cling to her, resisting her control. "We don't have time for experiments. We need to move."

He sighed, the faint glow of his flame dimming slightly, though the forest's energy still thrummed around them. "Fine, Eloryn. But one day, you'll see that there's strength in allowing things to be, without forcing them into boxes."

She shot him a wary look, her voice quiet but firm. "Control is what keeps us safe. Without it, everything falls apart."

"Is that what you think?" he asked, his tone thoughtful. "Or is it just what you've been taught to believe?"

She didn't answer, her gaze shifting to the path ahead, refusing to give him any more ground. But as they continued walking, the amplified sensation of their powers lingered in the air, pressing against her carefully constructed defenses, making her wonder—just for a fleeting moment—if there was truth in his words.

As they continued through the thickening mist, the forest seemed to close in around them, its presence more palpable than ever. Shadows clung to the trees, twisting and shifting with each step, while tendrils of mist curled around their ankles, tugging gently, as if urging them to pause, to pay attention to something beyond the physical world.

Lyra walked slightly ahead, her posture tense, every instinct telling her to maintain her distance from Kian. But the strange, almost magnetic energy of the forest made that difficult. The air between them felt charged, each step pulling them closer, like two opposing forces compelled by an invisible hand. She forced herself to stay focused, eyes trained forward, but she could feel his presence beside her, closer than before, his movements nearly in sync with hers.

"This forest," Kian murmured, his voice soft, cutting through the silence. "It's… intense tonight. Feels like it's trying to tell us something."

She scoffed, keeping her gaze forward. "The forest is always intense. It doesn't need a reason."

"Maybe," he said, not quite convinced. "But I've walked through a lot of forests, and this one feels… different. Almost as if it's alive."

She glanced at him, unable to help herself. "Of course it's alive. It's the Forest of Reflections. It reacts to people, to their energy. That's what makes it dangerous."

"Dangerous?" He smiled, his tone playful. "Or maybe just… perceptive."

She frowned, shifting her focus back to the path, trying to ignore the warmth in his gaze. "I don't have time for philosophy, Kian. The forest is what it is. Nothing more."

He laughed softly, the sound carrying a strange warmth in the cold air. "You say that, but you're as affected as I am. I can see it." He leaned in slightly, his tone teasing yet somehow gentle. "Doesn't it make you wonder what it's trying to tell us?"

"Nothing worth listening to," she replied, keeping her tone steady, but her words felt weak, even to her. The forest's strange energy was clouding her focus, pulling her thoughts in directions she didn't want to explore.

Kian looked at her, his gaze unwavering. "You can feel it too, can't you?" His voice dropped to a near whisper, laced with a rare sincerity that made her heart skip a beat. "This connection. The way the forest seems to… bring things to the surface."

She tensed, refusing to meet his gaze. "I don't feel anything," she said firmly, but the words felt like a lie, echoing hollowly in the thickened air.

He tilted his head, studying her with that infuriatingly calm expression. "You're a terrible liar, Lyra."

"Excuse me?" She spun to face him, her eyes narrowing, irritation flashing across her face. "I am not lying. I just don't get swept up in strange energies and vague feelings like you do."

"Really?" He raised an eyebrow, his smirk softening into something more genuine. "Because it seems to me like you're as caught up in this as I am. Maybe even more."

She clenched her fists, fighting the warmth creeping into her cheeks. "Believe what you want. I'm here to do my duty, not… not to entertain feelings or whatever it is you think this forest is trying to make us feel."

He took a small step closer, the shadows around them intensifying, almost as if responding to the tension between them. "Maybe that's the problem, Lyra," he said quietly. "Maybe the forest is showing us what we keep ignoring."

She forced herself to hold his gaze, though it took all her strength. "I'm not ignoring anything. I know exactly who I am and what I need to do."

"But do you know what you want?" he asked, his voice softer now, as if he were speaking directly to the part of her she kept hidden. "Or are you just following a path you didn't choose?"

She felt the question like a blow, striking at the carefully guarded core of her being. She opened her mouth to respond, but the words wouldn't come. Instead, she felt herself drawn to the depth in his eyes, the warmth there that felt like an invitation and a challenge all at once.

"This is absurd," she finally managed, tearing her gaze away, but her voice wavered, betraying the conflict brewing inside her. "The forest's energy is clouding your mind."

Kian chuckled, a knowing gleam in his eyes. "Maybe it's clouding both our minds." He hesitated, his voice dropping to a near whisper. "But what if that's the point?"

She looked at him, her guarded expression slipping for just a moment. "The point? What do you mean?"

He glanced around, as if the forest itself held answers he couldn't quite put into words. "This place—it's called the Forest of Reflections for a reason. Maybe it's trying to show us something about ourselves. About… what we're avoiding."

"Stop." Her voice was firm, but he had already seen the flicker of doubt in her eyes, and she knew it. She took a steadying breath, trying to push down the strange sensations rising within her. "I don't need reflections. I need focus. That's what matters."

Kian sighed, stepping back slightly, though his gaze remained steady, gentle. "I'm not trying to distract you, Lyra. I just… I see how hard you work to keep everything locked down. And maybe—just maybe—it doesn't have to be that way."

She shook her head, refusing to let his words reach her. "I don't expect you to understand. You live without rules, without duty. I can't afford that kind of… freedom."

"Maybe not," he said, his tone accepting, yet still laced with that quiet intensity. "But it doesn't mean you have to be alone in everything."

Silence settled between them, thick and charged. She felt the forest pressing in around her, the shadows deepening, the air heavier, almost as if it were echoing the unspoken words between them. She wanted to argue, to dismiss his words as foolishness, but there was a part of her—a small, quiet part—that wondered if he was right.

Finally, she spoke, her voice barely audible. "You don't know anything about me."

Kian's gaze softened, his expression gentle. "Maybe not everything. But I know enough to see that there's more to you than duty and discipline." He hesitated, then added, "And maybe it's time you saw it too."

She closed her eyes briefly, fighting the emotions welling up inside her, the strange, undeniable pull she felt toward him, as if the forest itself were amplifying every unacknowledged feeling she kept locked away. When she opened her eyes, she forced her tone back to its usual control.

"Stop talking like you know me," she whispered, her voice wavering slightly.

He gave her a sad smile, taking one last step back. "One day, maybe you'll let someone in enough to see you, Lyra. Really see you." His voice was gentle, devoid of its usual playfulness. "And I hope you'll be ready for it."

Before she could respond, he turned, disappearing into the mist once more, leaving her standing alone, her heart pounding, her mind a chaotic whirl of emotions she couldn't—wouldn't—name. The forest seemed to breathe with her, each rustle of leaves, each shift in the shadows echoing the turmoil she fought to suppress.

She took a shaky breath, forcing herself to calm down, but his words lingered, the warmth of his gaze haunting her thoughts. The forest felt alive around her, as if reflecting the truth she wasn't ready to face.

She whispered to herself, almost as if to the forest, "I don't need anyone to see me."

But even as she resumed her path, the words felt hollow, lost in the mist, like a lie spoken into the depths of the forest that refused to believe it. --------

The forest had quieted around them, the mist hanging low, weaving between the trees like a shroud. Lyra walked a few paces ahead, trying to ignore the persistent presence of Kian at her side. She felt the weight of everything they'd just experienced pressing down on her, and the forest's strange energy seemed to amplify the turmoil in her mind, making it harder to maintain her usual composure.

Kian matched her pace, his steps light but steady. He watched her carefully, an expression of quiet curiosity on his face, as if he could sense that something within her had shifted.

"You look… distracted," he said gently, his tone uncharacteristically soft.

She hesitated, unwilling to meet his gaze. "I'm just… thinking," she replied, her voice barely above a whisper.

"Thinking?" He raised an eyebrow, his expression turning thoughtful. "About what?"

She clenched her fists, wrestling with herself. The last thing she wanted was to reveal anything personal to him. But the forest seemed to press on her, amplifying the silence between them, urging her to speak. For a fleeting moment, the weight of her own thoughts, of the doubts she'd kept buried, became too much.

"Do you ever wonder…" she began, her voice barely audible, "if all this—the discipline, the rules—if it's really… worth it?"

Kian's eyes softened, his curiosity shifting into something gentler, more understanding. "Worth it?" he repeated, his voice encouraging. "What do you mean?"

She looked away, her gaze fixed on the shadowed path ahead. "I've dedicated everything to my clan, to their safety, to duty. It's what I've known my entire life." She paused, her voice wavering. "But sometimes… sometimes it feels like I'm losing something. Like there's a part of me I can't reach anymore."

He stepped closer, his gaze steady, filled with a warmth that surprised her. "Lyra… you don't always have to choose between duty and yourself. They don't have to be opposites."

Her breath hitched, the vulnerability of the moment pressing down on her. She glanced at him, the conflict in her eyes clear, a mix of frustration and yearning. "It's not that simple, Kian. I don't get to live freely, like you. I have responsibilities, expectations."

"I know," he replied quietly, his voice laced with empathy. "But it doesn't mean you have to lock away who you are."

She frowned, the tension building within her, a battle between the safety of her discipline and the quiet, unfamiliar desire to open up. "You don't understand," she whispered, almost to herself. "I've spent my whole life proving that I'm strong enough, that I can handle anything. If I let even one weakness slip through, it all falls apart."

Kian shook his head, his gaze steady and kind. "Strength doesn't mean shutting everyone out, Lyra. Sometimes it means letting yourself feel, letting yourself be… human."

She let out a hollow laugh, crossing her arms defensively. "Being human isn't what keeps people safe. Discipline is what keeps me safe."

"But at what cost?" he asked softly, his voice probing yet gentle. "How long can you keep carrying this alone?"

She faltered, his question striking deeper than she wanted to admit. A flicker of something unguarded, something painfully honest, slipped through her defenses. "Sometimes, I don't know," she murmured, barely realizing she'd spoken aloud. "Sometimes, it feels like… like I'm holding onto something that doesn't even belong to me."

He reached out, his hand hovering near her arm but not quite touching, as if he understood that even the smallest connection might tip her over the edge. "Then maybe it's time to figure out what does belong to you."

His words hung in the air, heavy and poignant, and for a brief, fragile moment, she felt the walls she'd built around herself begin to tremble. She looked at him, her guard slipping, her eyes filled with questions she couldn't bring herself to ask.

But then, as quickly as the vulnerability had surfaced, she pushed it back down, locking it away. She straightened, her posture snapping back into its usual rigidity. "No," she said, her voice hardening. "I can't afford to be uncertain. My duty is to my clan, to their protection. That's all that matters."

Kian's gaze didn't waver, but there was a hint of sadness in his eyes, as if he could see the effort it took for her to reassert her control. "And what about you, Lyra? Don't you matter too?"

She looked away, her jaw tightening. "What I want doesn't matter," she replied, her voice cold. "Not when lives are at stake."

He watched her, his expression unreadable, a mix of empathy and regret. "I think you believe that," he said softly. "But one day, Lyra, you'll have to face yourself. Not your duty, not your clan's expectations—just you."

The words lingered, piercing through her carefully constructed defenses, and she felt a pang of something she couldn't quite name. But instead of responding, she turned away, her steps resolute as she walked back toward the deeper shadows of the forest.

"Kian," she said, her voice firm, her back to him, "thank you for… listening." She hesitated, as if those words had cost her more than she wanted to admit. "But this is where I go on alone."

He nodded slowly, though she couldn't see him. "If that's what you need," he replied quietly, a note of understanding in his tone. "But just know… I'll be around. If you ever want company."

She didn't turn back, didn't give him any indication that his offer meant something, even if a part of her, buried deep, felt its warmth. Instead, she strode into the mist, her movements precise and controlled, each step reinforcing the walls she'd let slip only moments before.

Kian stood there, watching her disappear into the shadows, his expression thoughtful, the glint of curiosity still in his eyes. He could sense her resistance, her reluctance to let anyone close, yet something in her had softened, if only for a moment. He found himself wondering if the forest's magic had shown him a glimpse of the true Lyra—the one hidden beneath her duty and discipline.

He murmured to himself, his gaze still on the path she'd taken. "There's more to you than you realize, Lyra. And one day, I hope you'll see it too."

With a sigh, he turned and melted into the mist, the memory of her fleeting vulnerability lingering, a quiet reminder of the connection the forest had brought to the surface, despite her best efforts to keep it hidden.

Chapter 5
Reflections and Revelations

The forest around Lyra grew denser as she ventured deeper into its shadows, her steps quiet but purposeful. Each tree seemed older, their trunks thick and gnarled, their branches reaching out like twisted arms. There was a stillness here, a silence so profound that it felt like the forest was holding its breath, watching her every movement. She felt a faint prickle of unease, an awareness that something within this part of the forest was different, older, almost sentient.

As she moved further, a strange sensation washed over her—a faint pull, a tingling in the back of her mind. She blinked, feeling her vision blur slightly, as if she were slipping into a trance. And then, without warning, the world around her shifted, melting away into something familiar yet distant.

She was no longer in the depths of the forest; instead, she found herself standing in a clearing, a training ground from her youth. The air was filled with the sounds of clashing weapons, shouts of encouragement and correction from her mentors, and the rhythmic thud of footsteps on the packed earth.

She felt a jolt of recognition as she looked around, her heart pounding with the sudden intensity of the memory. "This… this can't be real," she whispered, her voice barely audible in the strange echo of the past.

But even as she tried to resist, the memory pulled her in deeper, surrounding her with images she hadn't thought of in years.

Her younger self was there, in the middle of the training ground, her stance focused, her expression set in the fierce determination of youth. She was sparring with one of her mentors, each movement precise, her strikes calculated. Every mistake, every misstep, was met with a sharp correction, a reminder that discipline was everything.

"Focus, Lyra," her mentor's voice rang out, firm and unyielding. "Discipline is what separates a warrior from a novice. Without it, you're nothing."

She watched herself nod, her young face tight with concentration, her grip on her practice sword tightening as she resumed her stance. There was no room for doubt in her gaze, no hint of hesitation. This was the path she had chosen, the only path she knew.

"Discipline is everything," her younger self repeated, her voice steady, her eyes unwavering.

The words echoed around her, mingling with the shadows of the forest, and she felt a strange weight settle on her chest. She had always believed that, always clung to the certainty of her training, her duty. But now, as she watched her younger self, a flicker of doubt crept into her mind, a question that felt like a crack in her armor.

"What if it's not everything?" she murmured, almost as if challenging the memory itself.

The vision shifted, and she found herself in another memory, one she had nearly forgotten. She was older now, just barely out of her teens, her stance more confident but her gaze harder, colder. She was in a quiet clearing, standing beside her mentor once more. They watched the sun dip below the horizon, casting long shadows across the ground.

"Lyra," her mentor had said, his voice softened with something that almost sounded like pride. "You're one of the most disciplined warriors I've ever trained. But remember, discipline can also be a cage. Sometimes, we build walls so strong that we trap ourselves inside them."

She remembered the confusion she'd felt, the way his words had unsettled her. "Discipline keeps us safe," she had replied, almost as if reciting a lesson. "It's what gives us strength."

Her mentor had sighed, looking at her with a mixture of sadness and understanding. "Strength is not the same as freedom, Lyra. One day, you may have to choose which matters more."

The memory faded, his words hanging in the air like a whisper, and she felt a pang of something she couldn't quite name—a mixture of loss and longing, a sense of something she had missed, something vital.

As she blinked, the forest around her returned, the mist curling around the trees, but the echoes of the past lingered, their weight heavy in her mind. She took a steadying breath, trying to shake off the strange, lingering sensation, the flood of emotions the forest had pulled from her memories.

"What is this place?" she whispered, as if the forest itself might answer.

"You look... distracted," came a voice from behind her.

She turned quickly, and there was Kian, leaning casually against a tree, his gaze curious, though there was a hint of concern in his eyes. "Didn't mean to intrude, but you seemed... somewhere else."

Lyra hesitated, her hand going instinctively to her blade, even though she knew she didn't need it. "The forest," she said, her voice low, almost hesitant. "It's... it's showing me things. Memories. Moments I thought I'd left behind."

Kian raised an eyebrow, taking a step closer. "Memories, huh? The Forest of Reflections is living up to its name, then."

She nodded, feeling a strange urge to confide in him, even as she fought to keep her walls intact. "It's unsettling," she admitted. "The way it brings up things you thought were buried."

He nodded, his gaze softening. "Sometimes, the things we bury are the things that need the most attention." He paused, studying her. "What did it show you?"

She looked away, unwilling to meet his gaze. "Moments from training. Lessons on discipline, on strength. Things I thought were the foundation of who I am."

He watched her for a moment, then spoke, his tone gentle. "And now?"

She clenched her jaw, struggling to find the words. "Now... I don't know. Seeing it all like this... it makes me wonder. Wonder if I've built walls so high that I've shut out everything else."

Kian's gaze softened further, a warmth in his eyes that felt both comforting and unnerving. "Sometimes, the strongest walls are the ones we need to break down. Just because something kept you safe once doesn't mean it's what you need forever."

She felt a pang of vulnerability, an unsteady feeling that made her want to retreat, to hide. But the forest seemed to press in around them, amplifying her emotions, keeping her from slipping back into her defenses.

"Discipline is all I've ever known," she whispered, her voice barely audible. "Without it... I don't know who I am."

Kian stepped closer, his gaze steady. "Maybe it's time to find out. Maybe there's more to you than just the duty you've been trained to follow."

She looked at him, a faint flicker of hope mixing with her uncertainty. "And what if there's nothing else? What if this... this is all I am?"

He smiled, his tone gentle yet firm. "I don't believe that for a second. And deep down, neither do you."

She held his gaze, feeling the weight of his words settle over her, stirring something she hadn't allowed herself to feel. But before she could respond, the forest shifted around them, the mist swirling as if it sensed the moment slipping away.

Lyra took a step back, her walls sliding back into place, her expression hardening. "I have to go," she said quickly, her voice firm. "I can't... I can't get distracted."

Kian nodded, though the look in his eyes told her he saw through her retreat. "Then go. But remember, Lyra, the past doesn't have to define you. You have the power to choose what comes next."

She turned, disappearing into the mist without another word, his words echoing in her mind as she walked, the memories of her past blending with the forest's whispers, haunting her steps.

Lyra moved cautiously through the dense trees, the lingering effects of the forest's visions still weighing on her mind. She tried to focus, to shake off the disorienting memories that clung to her like shadows. But no matter how hard she tried, the echoes of her past lingered, stirring questions she wasn't ready to confront. The forest seemed to close in around her, the mist thickening, its tendrils brushing against her as if aware of her turmoil.

Suddenly, a figure emerged from the fog just ahead, his movements as casual as if he'd simply been waiting for her to arrive. Kian leaned against a tree, his expression light, though his eyes held a glint of something sharper, more perceptive than his usual carefree demeanor.

"Are you stalking me now?" Lyra's tone was sharp, though her voice wavered slightly, betraying her lingering unease.

He grinned, unfazed. "If I were, I'd have done a better job staying hidden." He took a few steps closer, his gaze sweeping over her as if assessing her state. "You look like you've seen a ghost."

She scoffed, crossing her arms defensively. "This forest has a way of... showing things best left buried."

Kian nodded thoughtfully, his gaze shifting to the trees around them. "I know. The Forest of Reflections isn't exactly known for its subtlety. But I'd say that's part of its charm."

"Charm?" She shot him a withering look. "Is that what you call it?"

He shrugged, the faint hint of a smile tugging at his lips. "Maybe charm is the wrong word. But I can't help thinking that it reveals things for a reason. Like it's trying to teach us something."

She glanced away, unwilling to let his words resonate with her. "Or maybe it's just a forest full of old magic. Not everything has a hidden meaning, Kian."

"Maybe," he conceded, though his tone suggested he wasn't entirely convinced. "But given its reputation, traveling through it alone is… risky."

Lyra stiffened, instantly defensive. "I don't need anyone's help. I can handle myself."

He held up his hands, palms out, his expression amused. "I'm not saying you can't. But even the best warriors can get lost here. This forest has a way of… bending the rules. And if it's showing you things you didn't ask to see, maybe having someone else around could be helpful."

She narrowed her eyes, her gaze sharp and assessing. "You just want an excuse to tag along."

He grinned, unbothered by her accusation. "Maybe. Or maybe I'd rather not leave you alone in a place that's clearly getting under your skin."

She took a steadying breath, struggling to ignore the nagging pull of his suggestion. The forest's unpredictable nature was unsettling, especially with the way it had dredged up visions from her past. She didn't want to admit it, but traveling with someone else—even someone as irritating as Kian—might make the journey through the forest more bearable.

She shook her head, trying to keep her voice steady. "I don't need company. I'm used to traveling alone."

"I'm sure you are," he replied, his tone gentle but insistent. "But there's a difference between choosing solitude and letting it choose you." He paused, glancing around as if listening to the forest's whispers. "And something tells me this place has more in store for us. Wouldn't it be better to face it together?"

Lyra hesitated, her gaze dropping to the ground. The memories the forest had shown her had unsettled her more than she cared to admit. She couldn't deny the strange pull she felt, the sense that the forest was leading her toward something she hadn't yet seen. And as much as she hated to admit it, Kian's presence might provide a buffer, a distraction from the relentless reflections the forest seemed determined to show her.

She exhaled slowly, her voice reluctant. "Fine. But don't get in my way."

He smirked, clearly pleased, though he kept his tone light. "Wouldn't dream of it. I'll even let you lead, Eloryn."

She shot him a glare. "This isn't about letting you tag along so you can crack jokes. We're here for safety, nothing more."

He held her gaze, his expression softening, and for a moment, his usual lightheartedness gave way to something more serious. "Understood. But remember—sometimes, safety isn't just about keeping threats away. Sometimes, it's about having someone there when things get… difficult."

She looked away, his words hitting closer than she wanted to admit. The forest's visions had already begun to wear on her, leaving her feeling unsteady, her usual control slipping through her fingers. She didn't want to acknowledge the comfort of having someone nearby, but she couldn't deny that his presence eased some of the tension coiled inside her.

"Don't read into this," she said, her tone sharper than she intended. "I'm only agreeing because the forest has been... unpredictable. It's nothing personal."

Kian chuckled, a faint smile returning to his face. "Wouldn't dream of it. I'll be as quiet as a shadow if that's what you want."

"Good," she replied tersely, though she couldn't ignore the way his lighthearted response seemed to ease the weight on her chest.

They continued through the forest, the silence settling around them once more. She kept her gaze forward, her senses alert, but every so often, she could feel his presence beside her, steady and unobtrusive. Despite her reluctance, she found herself strangely reassured, a feeling that both unsettled and comforted her.

The trees grew denser as they walked, the mist thickening, and she felt the familiar pull of the forest's magic stirring again. Shadows danced at the edges of her vision, and faint whispers threaded through the air, words she couldn't quite make out but that stirred something deep within her.

Kian's voice broke the silence, soft but insistent. "Lyra... if the forest does show you something—something difficult—don't keep it all bottled up. I know you don't trust me, but that doesn't mean you have to carry everything alone."

She bristled, his words touching on a vulnerability she'd spent years burying. "I don't need anyone to carry anything for me."

"I'm not saying you do," he replied calmly, his gaze steady. "But sometimes, it helps to let someone else understand. Even if it's just for a moment."

She didn't respond, her jaw clenched, her gaze fixed on the path ahead. But his words lingered, settling into the quiet spaces in her mind. The forest was unpredictable, amplifying her memories, her emotions, pulling at parts of her she kept carefully hidden. And now, with Kian beside her, the barriers she'd constructed felt more fragile, as if the forest itself was encouraging her to let them fall.

Finally, she spoke, her voice barely a murmur. "If the forest does show me something... I don't expect you to understand."

He nodded, his expression gentle. "I won't pretend to understand everything. But I'm here. And sometimes, that's all it takes."

Lyra fell silent, unable to respond. They walked on, the forest wrapping around them like a cloak, but for the first time, she felt a faint sense of solace, a fragile connection that reminded her she wasn't entirely alone in the darkness.

Lyra and Kian moved cautiously through the thickening mist, the forest silent around them, as if it were waiting. The shadows had grown deeper, the trees taller and closer together, their twisted branches forming a dense canopy above. Every now and then, Lyra felt the weight of the forest pressing in on her, an almost sentient awareness that made her pulse quicken. She was used to the forest's magic by now, but this part of the forest felt different—older, more potent, as if it held secrets it was eager to reveal.

After a while, they reached a narrow clearing, the mist swirling around the edges. The trees here were different, their bark smooth and dark, reflecting a faint shimmer like polished glass. Lyra paused, her gaze sharpening as she took in the strange landscape, each tree casting distorted reflections that seemed to pulse and shift with an inner light.

Kian let out a soft whistle, his gaze sweeping over the trees. "Well, would you look at that," he murmured, taking a few steps forward, his hand grazing the bark of one tree. "They're… reflecting us."

Lyra stiffened, her instinct to retreat kicking in as she caught a glimpse of herself in the mirrored surface of a nearby tree. The reflection was strange, not quite aligned with her physical appearance. Instead of showing her face as it was, the image seemed to reflect something deeper, a shadowy outline of her emotions, her thoughts.

"Stay back," she said sharply, trying to keep her voice steady as she resisted the urge to look too closely. "This is forest magic, Kian. We don't know what it does."

He chuckled, unbothered by her caution. "Relax, Lyra. This might be the safest thing we've come across so far." He tilted his head, studying his own reflection, a faint grin on his face. "Look at this—it's like it's showing my emotions. Can you see it?"

She forced herself to look at his reflection, noting the vibrant flickers of light that seemed to emanate from his form in the mirrored bark. His face was calm, but the reflection showed something more—a warmth, an energy that pulsed and glowed, shifting with every movement he made.

"It's strange," she muttered, her gaze flickering between his reflection and his real form. "It's... like it's revealing parts of us we usually keep hidden."

Kian nodded, his expression thoughtful as he examined his own reflection, his features shifting in the faint glow. "Maybe the forest wants us to see ourselves differently. To face what we usually ignore."

Lyra tensed, her own reflection catching her attention again. Her mirrored image was dark, her figure outlined in a shifting shadow that seemed to pulse in time with her heartbeat. She could see flashes of her own emotions flickering across her reflection—doubt, tension, a vulnerability she kept buried. It was unsettling, seeing herself this way, exposed in a way that went beyond the physical.

"I don't like this," she said quietly, her voice edged with discomfort. "It feels... invasive."

Kian turned to her, a gentle smile playing on his lips. "Maybe that's the point. Sometimes, we need to see ourselves in a different light. It's not always comfortable, but it's part of understanding who we are."

She shot him a wary look, her tone defensive. "I don't need to understand myself through some magical reflection. I know who I am."

"Do you?" he asked, his gaze steady, his voice soft. "Or is it just who you think you have to be?"

Her fists clenched at her sides, the question striking a nerve. "I don't have time for this, Kian. We should keep moving."

He chuckled, his tone light but his eyes serious. "You're always so quick to turn away from anything uncomfortable. Maybe this forest is showing you what you've been avoiding."

She looked away, the reflection's pulsing shadows unsettling her as they seemed to deepen, drawing out emotions she fought to keep locked away. "Not everything needs to be examined, Kian. Some things are better left alone."

He sighed, a faint note of sadness slipping into his voice. "You think so, but maybe it's weighing on you more than you realize." He glanced back at his reflection, noting the vibrant glow around his form. "Look at me. It's like it's showing my energy, my curiosity. All the things that make me… me. It's kind of refreshing."

She couldn't help but feel a pang of envy at his ease, the way he seemed unbothered by the forest's probing magic. "That's because you have nothing to hide," she muttered, barely meeting his gaze.

He turned to her, his smile softening, his eyes gentle. "And neither should you, Lyra. There's strength in embracing who you are, in facing the parts of yourself that scare you."

She swallowed, her eyes flickering back to her own reflection. The shadows seemed darker now, more intense, swirling with fragments of thoughts, memories, insecurities she kept hidden even from herself. She could see hints of her past, glimpses of moments she'd fought hard to forget—losses, mistakes, times she'd felt weak or uncertain.

"Maybe… maybe I don't want to see it," she admitted quietly, almost to herself.

Kian reached out, his hand resting lightly on her shoulder. "You're stronger than you think, Lyra. Whatever this forest shows you… it's not meant to hurt you. Maybe it's giving you a chance to let go."

She stiffened under his touch, torn between retreating and the unexpected comfort his words brought. "I don't need to let go," she replied, though her voice lacked its usual conviction. "Control is what keeps me strong."

"Control is useful," he agreed, his tone thoughtful. "But sometimes, it's okay to let yourself feel. To allow yourself to be vulnerable, even if it's just to yourself."

She looked away, her gaze drifting to the shadows in her reflection, the way they seemed to pulse with her emotions, a silent reminder of the parts of herself she'd buried for so long. The sight unsettled her, but she couldn't deny that part of her was drawn to it, a faint desire to understand what the shadows held.

Kian stepped back, his hand slipping away, though his gaze remained warm, encouraging. "If it helps, I think the forest is trying to help us. Even if it's uncomfortable."

She shook her head, her jaw clenched. "Help or not, I don't need to indulge it. We should keep moving."

He watched her for a long moment, a look of understanding in his eyes. "Alright," he said finally, his voice gentle. "But maybe, when you're ready, you'll take a look. For yourself."

Without another word, she turned and continued along the path, her steps firm, but the image of her shadowy reflection lingered in her mind, haunting her with the unspoken truths it held. And though she wouldn't admit it, Kian's words echoed with a quiet insistence, stirring something within her that she could no longer ignore.

The forest remained silent as they continued, the mist swirling lazily around their feet, amplifying the strange atmosphere that seemed to cling to this part of the woods. Lyra kept her gaze fixed ahead, her mind wrestling with the visions she'd seen in the trees' reflections. She had always been certain, grounded in her beliefs and her duty. But here, in the heart of the Forest of Reflections, the certainty she'd clung to so fiercely felt... shaken.

Kian walked beside her, his steps light, his expression thoughtful. He seemed to sense the unease radiating from her, but he said nothing, letting the silence stretch between them. Lyra found herself both irritated by and oddly grateful for his quiet presence, though she would never admit it.

Finally, Kian broke the silence, his tone gentle. "You know, those reflections... they're not just tricks of the forest. They're showing us something real. Something we might not want to see."

She stiffened, her voice edged with irritation. "I don't need the forest to show me who I am. I already know."

"Do you?" He glanced at her, his gaze steady but probing. "Because from what I saw back there, it seems like there's more to you than you let on."

Her jaw clenched, and she quickened her pace. "You're imagining things, Kian. Just because you're comfortable letting the forest see into your mind doesn't mean I have to."

He sighed, but his voice remained calm, almost amused. "I'm not asking you to do anything, Lyra. But it seems to me that the forest is. Maybe it's time you listened."

She stopped abruptly, turning to face him, her eyes narrowed. "I don't need life lessons from you. I know what my strengths are. I know who I am."

Kian raised an eyebrow, unfazed by her defensive tone. "Knowing who you are and being willing to face every part of yourself—those aren't the same thing."

She crossed her arms, her expression cold. "And what would you know about it? You're a wanderer, drifting from place to place without purpose, without commitment. You don't understand what it means to carry the weight of duty."

He held her gaze, a hint of challenge in his eyes. "Maybe I don't. But I do understand that ignoring parts of yourself doesn't make them go away."

Lyra's shoulders tightened, the truth of his words hitting closer than she wanted to admit. She'd spent years honing her control, perfecting her discipline, locking away anything that might weaken her resolve. And yet, the forest had shown her the cracks in her armor, the shadows she'd kept hidden.

"It doesn't matter," she said finally, her voice quieter, almost as if she were trying to convince herself. "All that matters is my duty, my purpose. Feelings… they're just distractions."

Kian stepped closer, his tone softer but insistent. "Feelings are part of what make us who we are, Lyra. Ignoring them doesn't make you stronger. It just makes you… lonelier."

She scoffed, brushing off his words, though they settled uncomfortably in her mind. "I don't need anyone's company. I don't need… whatever it is you're trying to suggest."

He gave her a small, understanding smile. "I'm not suggesting anything, other than that maybe there's more to life than what you've let yourself believe."

She looked away, frustration simmering beneath her skin. "I don't have the luxury of wondering about 'more.' Duty doesn't leave room for those kinds of questions."

"Maybe not," he replied, his voice gentle but unwavering. "But that doesn't mean the questions aren't still there, waiting for you to face them."

She clenched her fists, the image of her shadowed reflection flashing in her mind, the way it had shown pieces of herself she barely recognized. Parts that were vulnerable, uncertain. Weak. The very things she'd worked so hard to bury.

"Enough," she said firmly, her voice sharper than she intended. "You don't understand, Kian. You've never had to answer to anyone, never had to sacrifice for something greater than yourself."

He sighed, his gaze softening, and for a moment, she thought she saw a flicker of sadness in his eyes. "Maybe that's true. But maybe that's why I can see what you're missing."

She shot him a glare, unwilling to let him reach the part of her that was beginning to question. "I'm not missing anything. I've chosen this path. I know what's required of me."

Kian studied her, his expression a mix of empathy and quiet challenge. "Sometimes, the hardest thing isn't choosing the path. It's realizing when the path is no longer serving you."

The words hung between them, heavy and unyielding, pressing against her carefully constructed walls. She wanted to dismiss him, to push his words away, but she couldn't shake the sense that there was a truth in what he was saying. The forest's reflections had already forced her to confront parts of herself she'd ignored, and now, Kian's words seemed to amplify the conflict growing within her.

"I don't need to change anything," she said finally, though her voice sounded weak, even to herself. "This is who I am. This is what I've trained for."

He nodded slowly, his gaze steady. "I get it, Lyra. But just because you're good at something doesn't mean it's the only thing you're meant for." He paused, then added softly, "And it doesn't mean you have to face it alone."

She swallowed, his words settling into the spaces in her heart she rarely acknowledged. But even as she felt the urge to consider what he was saying, to let herself imagine another way, she pushed it down, retreating back into the comfort of her discipline, her control.

"This conversation is pointless," she said, her tone firm once more. "We have a mission. That's all that matters right now."

Kian didn't respond immediately, but he nodded, his expression a mixture of acceptance and quiet disappointment. "Fine," he said finally, his voice gentle. "But just remember, Lyra… the forest has a way of bringing things to the surface, whether we're ready for them or not."

She didn't answer, turning away from him, her steps resolute as she continued down the path. But his words stayed with her, lingering in her mind, intertwining with the images of her reflection, the shadows that had revealed parts of herself she'd tried so hard to ignore.

As they walked, the silence between them felt charged, the weight of unspoken truths pressing down on her. And though she didn't look back, she couldn't shake the feeling that Kian's quiet presence was pulling her toward a truth she wasn't ready to face.

Chapter 6
Whispers of Doubt

As Lyra moved deeper into the forest, a heavy silence surrounded her, more oppressive than before. Each step felt weighted, as though the ground itself were urging her to pause, to linger. The mist had thickened, and the trees seemed to lean in closer, their darkened bark polished to a mirror-like sheen that caught flashes of her own reflection with every step. But now, something had shifted within her. The reflections she saw didn't just show her face; they seemed to flicker with emotions she'd spent years pushing down, shadows of doubt and hesitation dancing just behind her eyes.

Kian walked beside her, his presence uncharacteristically quiet. He seemed to sense the change in her, though he didn't say anything, merely watching her with a sidelong glance as they continued forward.

Lyra finally broke the silence, her voice barely above a whisper. "This forest… it's doing something. It's making me… question things I shouldn't be questioning."

He looked at her, his gaze curious. "What kind of things?"

She hesitated, not used to speaking so openly, especially with someone like him. But the forest's magic pressed in on her, its silent insistence peeling back layers she wasn't sure she could keep hidden anymore. "Things I've believed in my whole life. Duty. Discipline. The idea that… that I can't afford to let my guard down."

Kian nodded, his voice gentle. "And why can't you? Why does duty have to mean shutting yourself off from everything else?"

She glanced at him, her expression guarded. "Because that's what I was taught. That's what makes a person strong. Feelings… attachments… they make you vulnerable."

"But vulnerability isn't weakness, Lyra," he countered, his tone soft but firm. "Sometimes, it's where real strength comes from."

She let out a short, bitter laugh. "Spoken like someone who's never had to carry the weight of anyone else's expectations."

He raised an eyebrow, his expression thoughtful. "And is that what you feel? Like you're carrying the weight of others' expectations?"

She looked away, her gaze fixed on the misty path ahead. "It's more than just feeling, Kian. It's knowing. I have a duty, a purpose. The people who trained me… they expect me to be strong, to uphold what they've taught me. They don't… they don't understand anything else."

"And what about what you want?" he asked, his voice barely above a whisper.

Her jaw clenched, and she felt a flare of frustration. "I don't get to have what I want. This isn't about me."

Kian sighed, his tone understanding but unyielding. "Lyra, you're not just a weapon. You're a person. And pretending otherwise... maybe that's what this forest is trying to show you."

She stopped abruptly, turning to face him, her eyes narrowed. "What is it with you? Why do you keep pushing me like this?"

He met her gaze steadily. "Because I can see the struggle you're going through. And because I think there's more to you than this armor you wear. But you're the only one who can decide to let it down."

She shook her head, fighting the emotions his words stirred. "Letting my guard down means being weak, Kian. And if I'm weak, then I fail. I can't afford that."

He studied her for a long moment, his gaze intense. "Or maybe failing isn't about being weak. Maybe it's about losing yourself entirely to something that doesn't give anything back."

His words struck a chord she didn't want to acknowledge, and she turned away, staring into the shadows of the forest. The reflections in the trees seemed to shimmer, echoing her own doubts, her fears. She'd spent her life building walls, relying on discipline to define her, to keep her strong. But now, in this strange, sentient forest, the very things that had always grounded her felt fragile, like illusions she could no longer hold on to.

After a long silence, she murmured, almost to herself, "What if... what if I don't know who I am without it?"

Kian's voice was soft, a thread of understanding woven through his words. "Maybe that's what this journey is really about. Figuring out who you are, beyond what's been drilled into you."

She swallowed, her throat tight. "You make it sound so simple. Just… questioning everything I've ever known, everything I've sacrificed for."

He smiled gently, though his eyes were serious. "No one said it would be simple. But maybe it's necessary. Maybe that's why the forest brought you here."

She shook her head, resisting the pull of his words. "I don't want to question it. I need to be strong. That's what I was taught. That's what keeps me going."

"But Lyra," he said, his tone barely a whisper, "are you living for the strength others expect, or are you finding strength in yourself?"

She felt her defenses waver, a crack in the armor she'd held onto for so long. "I don't know," she admitted quietly. "I've never let myself think about it."

"Then maybe it's time," he replied, his gaze unwavering. "Maybe it's time to find out what's really in your heart, not just what others put there."

Her pulse quickened, the weight of his words pressing down on her, stirring something deep within her that she hadn't let herself feel in years. She took a deep, steadying breath, forcing herself to keep her voice steady.

"I'm not sure I know how," she whispered, her words slipping out before she could stop them.

Kian smiled, a warmth in his gaze that felt like reassurance. "You don't have to know everything right now. Just... be willing to see what's there. The rest will come in time."

She stared at him, caught between her fierce loyalty to her past and the quiet, unspoken desire to understand herself beyond the walls she'd built. But as much as she wanted to retreat, to dismiss his words, she couldn't deny that something in her had shifted. The forest's quiet influence, coupled with Kian's persistence, was breaking through her defenses, forcing her to confront a truth she'd long avoided.

Finally, she nodded, a hesitant acceptance she wasn't yet ready to put into words. She started walking again, her steps slower, more thoughtful, her mind filled with questions she couldn't ignore.

And as Kian fell into step beside her, she couldn't shake the feeling that, for the first time, she wasn't entirely alone in the forest.

The mist had thinned slightly as they continued down the narrow, winding path, the trees towering around them, their branches casting long shadows that stretched across the forest floor. Lyra kept her gaze forward, her steps precise, but Kian's presence beside her felt like a gentle, persistent pressure. She had expected his usual banter, but instead, he seemed unusually thoughtful, his silence almost contemplative.

After a while, he broke the silence, his voice quiet yet filled with a strange warmth. "You know… this forest reminds me of a place back home."

Lyra glanced at him, curiosity flickering in her eyes despite her efforts to remain indifferent. "Back home?"

He nodded, his gaze distant, as if he were looking back through years rather than miles. "My clan… we don't have forests like this, exactly. But we have open plains, vast fields under endless skies. No boundaries, no walls. Freedom as far as you can see."

She raised an eyebrow, though she kept her tone even. "Sounds… undisciplined."

Kian chuckled, unbothered by her remark. "That's one way to put it. Discipline isn't really a word you'd hear often where I'm from. Freedom, on the other hand… that's sacred."

"Freedom?" she echoed, a hint of skepticism slipping into her voice. "How do you even protect something as vague as 'freedom'?"

He looked at her, his expression softening. "Freedom isn't vague to us, Lyra. It's everything. The right to choose, to live by our own rules. To be who we want to be, not who we're told to be."

Lyra's gaze sharpened, her voice cool. "And what happens when everyone wants something different? When there's no order?"

Kian shrugged, a smile tugging at the corners of his mouth. "It works itself out. People find their way. We learn to adapt to each other, to give each other space. There's a kind of... harmony in the chaos."

"Harmony in chaos." She scoffed, shaking her head. "That sounds dangerous. Without rules, without structure, how can you trust anyone to do what's right?"

"That's the thing," he replied, his tone thoughtful. "We trust each other because we have the freedom to be ourselves. It's not about control—it's about respect. There's a bond, an understanding that no one will try to cage the other. We might be different, but we learn to live with each other's differences. Sometimes, that's stronger than any rule or law."

Lyra looked away, a flicker of something unreadable in her eyes. "It sounds... unpredictable."

"Maybe it is." He shrugged again, his voice light. "But that's part of the beauty. Freedom has a way of bringing out parts of people they wouldn't show otherwise. In a way, it's the purest form of trust."

She shook her head, her tone edged with skepticism. "Trust alone isn't enough. People need discipline. Without it, they become reckless, dangerous."

Kian smiled gently, though there was a hint of sadness in his gaze. "Or maybe… discipline makes them afraid to be themselves. Maybe it cages parts of them they don't even realize they've hidden."

She felt a pang of something—unease, intrigue, she wasn't sure which. But she kept her voice steady, dismissive. "People need limits, Kian. Freedom might work in your clan, but discipline is what holds ours together."

He studied her for a moment, his gaze soft but unyielding. "Is that what you believe? Or is that what you were told to believe?"

Lyra bristled, her gaze hardening. "It's not about belief. It's fact. Discipline keeps us safe, keeps us strong. Without it, we'd fall apart."

"Would you?" he asked, his voice gentle but insistent. "Or is that what you've been taught to fear?"

Her jaw tightened, his question striking a nerve she hadn't realized was there. She took a steadying breath, forcing herself to remain composed. "Fear has nothing to do with it. Discipline is a choice. It's what we're taught to value."

Kian nodded, his expression understanding but unconvinced. "I'm not saying discipline doesn't have value. I'm just saying… maybe there's more to strength than control. Maybe there's strength in letting go, even if just a little."

She looked away, her tone cold. "Letting go is a luxury. And it's one I can't afford."

They walked in silence for a moment, the air thick with unspoken tension. Finally, Kian spoke, his voice barely more than a whisper. "You know, Lyra... I think there's a part of you that wants to believe in freedom. Even if you won't admit it."

She shot him a look, her eyes flashing with irritation. "You don't know anything about me, Kian. Don't pretend you do."

He smiled softly, a hint of warmth in his gaze. "Maybe I don't know everything. But I see enough to know that there's more to you than just duty and discipline. Maybe there's a part of you that longs for something else. Something more."

Her steps faltered, his words slipping past her defenses in a way she hadn't expected. She kept her gaze forward, her voice tight. "What I long for doesn't matter. My purpose is clear, and that's all I need."

"Is it?" he asked quietly, his gaze unwavering. "Or is it just all you've ever allowed yourself to believe?"

She fell silent, the question lingering in her mind, weaving itself into the doubts the forest had already stirred. But as much as his words unsettled her, she forced herself to hold on to her resolve, the walls she'd built over years of training and duty.

Without looking back, she walked ahead, her expression steeled, even as a faint whisper of curiosity and doubt trailed behind her, waiting for her to finally acknowledge it.

The mist thickened around them as they ventured deeper into the forest. Lyra's senses sharpened, an instinctual wariness settling over her. She kept her hand near her blade, feeling the air shift, charged with something dark and alive. Beside her, Kian moved with an easy confidence, though she could see his eyes scanning the surroundings, alert and prepared.

Then, just ahead, a shadow shifted, detaching itself from the darkened underbrush and coalescing into a shape that made her heart quicken. It was a creature unlike any she'd seen before—its form shifting, insubstantial, with flickering eyes like smoldering embers that seemed to pierce through the mist.

Without a word, she and Kian fell into a fighting stance, moving in unison. The creature let out a low, guttural growl, its form expanding, tendrils of darkness stretching toward them, weaving through the mist like grasping fingers.

"Stay sharp," Kian muttered, his gaze locked on the creature. "This thing doesn't look like it's here to chat."

Lyra gave a terse nod, her focus unyielding. "Just don't get in my way."

He smirked, though his expression remained tense. "Wouldn't dream of it."

The creature lunged forward, its shadowy limbs lashing out with speed and precision. Instinctively, Lyra and Kian moved in harmony, their actions flowing together as if choreographed.

Lyra struck first, her blade slicing through the mist, her shadows deepening around her, amplifying her power. As she moved, she felt a surge of energy, a strange connection that linked her actions with Kian's, an unspoken coordination that allowed them to maneuver around the creature with ease.

Kian's flames flared to life beside her, bright and fierce, his movements mirroring hers. He sidestepped a shadowy limb, his fire casting a warm glow that melded with her shadows, strengthening their combined presence. She could feel his energy, his focus, as if his very Self was feeding into her own, intensifying the power they wielded.

For a brief moment, the creature faltered, its form wavering under the combined assault. Lyra felt the strange synergy between them, an almost electric bond that amplified her shadows, grounding her power in a way she hadn't anticipated.

"Do you feel that?" Kian's voice cut through the tension, his tone both surprised and exhilarated. "It's like… our powers are aligning."

She hesitated, her grip tightening on her blade. "I feel it… but I don't understand it."

He met her gaze, his eyes bright with an intensity that sent a shiver through her. "Maybe it doesn't need to be understood. Maybe it's just… right."

The creature let out a furious shriek, its form shifting, attempting to regroup. Without thinking, Lyra and Kian struck in unison, their attacks synchronized, her shadows and his flames intertwining, creating a barrier of light and darkness that seemed to disorient their foe. It stumbled back, retreating into the mist, its flickering eyes narrowing in frustration.

As they moved, Lyra felt herself instinctively attuned to Kian's every motion, every shift in his stance. She knew when he was about to strike, and he seemed to anticipate her moves, their energies feeding off each other, growing stronger with every coordinated attack.

"This connection…" she murmured, more to herself than to him, "I've never felt anything like it."

Kian glanced at her, a slight smile softening his expression. "It's because you've never let yourself feel it. You've always fought alone."

She frowned, his words unsettling her even as the truth of them echoed within her. "Fighting alone has always worked for me."

"But look at what we're capable of together," he countered, his voice low, as though they were sharing a secret. "Doesn't this feel… right?"

The creature lunged again, its shadowed limbs striking with renewed aggression, but Lyra and Kian moved as one, her shadows blending seamlessly with his flames, creating a protective shield that deflected the attack. She could feel the strength of their combined powers surging through her, intensifying her senses, sharpening her focus.

But even as the connection bolstered her, something held her back, a hesitation rooted in the discipline she'd always clung to. "This… it's dangerous," she said, her voice strained, almost as if she were speaking to herself.

Kian gave her a quick look, his voice steady. "Sometimes the things that scare us are the very things that make us stronger."

She clenched her jaw, struggling with the truth of his words. "Strength isn't about relying on someone else. It's about control."

"Maybe it used to be," he replied, deflecting a shadowy strike with a wave of his flames. "But we're stronger together, Lyra. You can feel it. Why fight that?"

The creature shrieked again, its form wavering, disoriented under the relentless assault of their combined powers. Lyra watched as her shadows darkened, lacing through his flames, enhancing them, transforming them into something new, something powerful.

"I'm not used to this," she admitted, her voice barely a whisper. "I don't… I don't know how to trust it."

Kian's gaze softened, though his stance remained steady. "Then just trust yourself. Trust what you're feeling right now, in this moment."

The creature made one last, desperate lunge, but with a final, powerful strike, Lyra and Kian moved together, their powers colliding with the creature's form, shattering it into fragments that dissipated into the mist. The silence that followed was thick, almost reverent, as though the forest itself were holding its breath.

They stood there, breathing heavily, the echoes of the fight fading around them. Lyra glanced at Kian, her expression unreadable, though her eyes held a flicker of something new—an unspoken question, a hint of wonder she couldn't quite ignore.

Kian met her gaze, a quiet satisfaction in his expression. "See? Together, we're stronger than anything we face alone."

She looked away, her voice quiet but resolute. "I'm still not sure I trust it."

He smiled, a hint of understanding in his gaze. "Maybe trust doesn't come all at once. But it has to start somewhere."

They resumed their path in silence, but Lyra couldn't shake the feeling that something had shifted within her, a faint, almost imperceptible change that she wasn't ready to name. The forest watched them in quiet approval, as if acknowledging the small but significant step she'd taken. And though she held onto her caution, a part of her couldn't deny that, for the first time, she'd felt something more than just her own strength.

The silence settled around them as the mist slowly lifted, and the echoes of the battle faded into the depths of the forest. Lyra sheathed her blade, the adrenaline still pulsing through her veins, but her mind felt unsettled, the weight of what had just happened pressing down on her. She could still feel the strange, lingering connection from fighting alongside Kian, his flames merging with her shadows. It had felt... right, in a way she couldn't explain but couldn't deny either.

Kian looked at her, his eyes filled with that familiar mixture of curiosity and challenge. "You know, that was incredible back there," he began, his tone light but edged with something deeper. "I didn't know we could fight like that—together."

She brushed him off, her voice cool. "It was nothing more than necessity. The forest threw something at us, and we dealt with it. That's all."

Kian raised an eyebrow, not buying her dismissal. "Is that really all it was? Because it looked like more than just necessity to me. It felt like... trust."

Her gaze hardened. "Trust has nothing to do with it. We were just doing what needed to be done."

"Needed to be done?" He shook his head, a faint smile on his lips. "Lyra, do you hear yourself? You talk like you're some kind of machine, like there's nothing to this but duty and discipline."

"Because there isn't." She crossed her arms, her tone defensive. "Duty is what keeps me focused. It's what matters."

Kian sighed, looking at her with an expression that bordered on exasperated affection. "Duty is important, yes. But it's not everything, Lyra. There's more to life than following orders and keeping your emotions in check."

Her eyes narrowed, irritation flaring. "Not for me. That's not how I was raised, and it's not how things work for my clan."

He took a step closer, his gaze softening as he searched her face. "And do you ever wonder if there's more? If maybe the strict values you were raised with aren't the only way?"

She met his gaze head-on, though the question struck deeper than she wanted to admit. "I don't have the luxury to wonder, Kian. Discipline, focus—those are the things that keep people safe."

"But at what cost?" he pressed, his voice gentle but firm. "You're so focused on your duty that you're shutting out everything else. Even yourself."

Her jaw clenched, and she looked away, unwilling to let him see the faint crack his words had caused in her resolve. "You don't understand," she replied, her voice strained. "Discipline is what gives me strength. It's what keeps me… grounded."

Kian studied her for a moment, his expression thoughtful. "Strength isn't just about control, Lyra. It's also about being open to… I don't know, change. Or even connection. You don't have to shut everything out to be strong."

She scoffed, dismissing him. "That might work for you and your clan of free spirits, but it's different for us. We don't have the luxury of living without rules."

He sighed, running a hand through his hair. "Lyra, just because you were taught something doesn't mean it's the only way. Doesn't mean it's even the right way for you."

She bristled, a mixture of frustration and discomfort rising within her. "You don't know what you're talking about. Duty isn't a choice—it's a responsibility. It's… it's who I am."

Kian's gaze softened, and he lowered his voice, as if coaxing her into an honesty she wasn't ready for. "And if you weren't bound by duty? If it was just you… who would you be?"

The question left her momentarily speechless. She felt a flicker of something unsettling, a hint of fear mixed with longing that she quickly tried to suppress. "I don't know," she muttered, barely audible. "And it doesn't matter."

He took a step closer, his tone gentle but insistent. "But it does matter. Because it's not about abandoning duty, Lyra. It's about letting yourself be more than just a soldier."

She held her ground, refusing to let his words reach the part of her that was already wavering. "I don't need to be anything more. This is who I am."

Kian shook his head, a sad smile tugging at his lips. "You don't believe that. Not really. I can see it in your eyes. You're questioning everything you've been told, but you're too afraid to admit it."

"Afraid?" she scoffed, though her voice lacked its usual bite. "I'm not afraid of anything."

"Aren't you?" He looked at her with a quiet intensity, his voice barely more than a whisper. "Maybe you're not afraid of the forest or the shadows we fought. But I think you're terrified of letting yourself feel… anything."

She felt her chest tighten, a rush of emotions pushing against the walls she'd built. "I don't have time for feelings, Kian. I have a duty to fulfill, people who depend on me."

"But who's there for you, Lyra?" he asked softly, his gaze unwavering. "Who's there when you need someone?"

She didn't answer, her gaze fixed on the ground, her mind racing. The forest seemed to watch them, silent and knowing, amplifying her doubts, softening her resolve. The echoes of his words reverberated within her, stirring questions she'd long avoided.

Finally, she lifted her head, her voice barely steady. "Duty is… enough for me. It has to be."

Kian didn't push further, but the sadness in his eyes spoke volumes. "I think you're stronger than you realize, Lyra. And I think, one day, you'll see that strength isn't about shutting yourself off. It's about being willing to open up."

She shook her head, a part of her wanting to dismiss him, to reject the things he was saying. But another part, a quiet, insistent part, held on to his words, their truth settling uneasily in her heart.

Without another word, she turned and began walking down the path, her steps resolute, though her mind felt anything but. The forest's quiet influence continued to press on her, a soft, persistent reminder that perhaps there was more to strength than she'd ever allowed herself to consider.

Chapter 7
Mirror Lake

The mist parted slowly as Lyra stepped forward, her breath catching at the sight of Mirror Lake. The lake lay before her, still and dark, its surface smooth as glass, reflecting the towering trees and the sky's faint twilight glow. She'd heard of this place—an ancient, fabled lake in the heart of the forest, known to reveal truths that were hidden even from oneself.

She hesitated, her instincts flaring, every sense alert. The lake seemed to pulse with a quiet energy, an invitation and a warning wrapped into one. She could feel its presence pressing on her, a silent urging to come closer.

Kian stepped up beside her, his gaze sweeping over the lake with a look of awe. "So this is Mirror Lake. I've heard about it, but I didn't think it actually existed."

Lyra crossed her arms, trying to steady herself. "It's real," she replied, her voice low. "And they say it's dangerous."

He glanced at her, his eyes glinting with curiosity. "Dangerous how?"

She kept her gaze fixed on the lake. "They say it reveals things... things about yourself you might not want to see."

Kian chuckled softly, though his expression remained serious. "That doesn't sound dangerous. That sounds... enlightening."

She shot him a look, her tone edged with irritation. "For someone like you, maybe. For the rest of us, it's more complicated."

"Complicated?" He raised an eyebrow, his voice softening. "Or just uncomfortable?"

She turned away, the unease in her chest tightening. "You wouldn't understand. You don't have anything to hide."

Kian tilted his head, studying her. "Everyone has something to hide, Lyra. Even me."

She looked at him, surprise flickering in her eyes. "I thought you were all about freedom and openness. Isn't that what your clan values?"

He nodded, a faint smile playing at his lips. "True. But that doesn't mean I don't have things I keep to myself. Sometimes freedom is about choosing what to share and what to hold back."

She frowned, turning back to the lake. "This isn't about choosing. The lake doesn't give you a choice. It shows you what's inside, whether you're ready for it or not."

Kian took a step closer, his gaze steady on her. "So what are you afraid it'll show you?"

Her jaw tightened, a flash of defiance in her eyes. "I'm not afraid. I just… don't see the point. I already know who I am."

He held her gaze, his tone soft but probing. "Do you? Because from what I've seen, there's a lot you haven't let yourself explore."

Lyra's fists clenched, her voice cold. "My life is about duty, Kian. Discipline. There's no room for… exploration."

"But this place," he said, nodding toward the lake, "it's giving you the chance to see more of yourself. To understand what you really want."

She shook her head, frustration and uncertainty swirling within her. "What I want doesn't matter. I have responsibilities, things I can't ignore just because of some mystical lake."

He sighed, his gaze softening. "Sometimes, understanding yourself makes you stronger, not weaker. Isn't that what you've been searching for? Strength?"

She didn't respond, her gaze fixed on the lake, the stillness of its surface unnerving. She could feel its pull, a gentle insistence that seemed to whisper to her, urging her to step forward.

Kian took another step closer, his voice barely more than a whisper. "Lyra, what's the worst thing it could show you?"

She exhaled slowly, her voice tight. "I don't know. That's the problem."

He gave her a reassuring smile. "Maybe it'll show you something you need. Something you didn't realize was missing."

She glanced at him, her defenses softening just slightly. "And what about you? Are you going to look?"

Kian nodded, his expression calm, though there was a hint of hesitation in his eyes. "I think I will. I've always believed in facing myself, even if it's not always easy."

Lyra bit her lip, her gaze drifting back to the lake. "And what if it shows you something you don't want to see?"

He shrugged, a faint smile tugging at his lips. "Then maybe that's exactly what I need to see."

She looked down, a flicker of doubt breaking through her resolve. The lake's quiet power pressed on her, the stillness of its surface inviting her to take that final step, to confront whatever lay hidden within herself.

Finally, she murmured, almost to herself, "I've spent my whole life focusing on what's expected of me. On duty, on discipline. What if there's nothing else?"

Kian's gaze softened, his voice filled with gentle assurance. "Then maybe the lake will show you something you never expected. Something that's been waiting inside you all along."

She looked at him, her expression vulnerable for just a moment. "It's not that easy, Kian."

"I know," he replied softly. "But you're stronger than you realize, Lyra. And facing yourself… it's part of that strength."

She took a steadying breath, her gaze lingering on the lake. "I don't know if I'm ready."

He placed a hand lightly on her shoulder, his touch grounding. "No one's ever really ready. But sometimes, you have to take the step anyway."

Lyra felt a quiet calm settle over her, Kian's words echoing in her mind as she took another tentative step closer to the lake. The stillness of the water seemed to deepen, drawing her in, a silent promise and challenge intertwined.

Lyra stood by the edge of Mirror Lake, her gaze fixed on its glassy surface but her feet rooted firmly to the ground. The water was so still, it was almost eerie, like a flawless mirror stretched out before her, reflecting the twilight-draped trees and darkening sky. Yet it wasn't the stillness that unnerved her. It was the knowledge of what the lake was capable of—the way it was said to show the truths one kept buried, secrets even the strongest walls couldn't hide.

She took a deep breath, steeling herself, but her resolve wavered as she felt the lake's quiet pull. Just then, she heard footsteps approaching behind her, and she didn't need to turn to know it was Kian.

"So… this is the legendary Mirror Lake," he said, his voice filled with a mix of curiosity and awe. He moved to stand beside her, his gaze drifting over the lake's surface. "I never thought I'd actually see it."

She forced herself to keep her expression neutral, her voice steady. "It's just a lake, Kian."

He raised an eyebrow, a hint of amusement in his eyes. "Just a lake that supposedly shows us the things we'd rather not face?"

"Legends are often exaggerated," she replied, trying to dismiss it, though the words sounded weak even to her own ears.

Kian chuckled softly, his gaze still fixed on the water. "Maybe. But then again, sometimes legends have a grain of truth. Aren't you just a little curious about what it might show?"

Lyra looked away, her jaw tightening. "Curiosity isn't the same as wisdom. Some things are better left unknown."

He turned to her, studying her with that familiar, probing gaze. "Are you sure? Or are you just afraid of what you might see?"

Her eyes flashed with irritation, though she kept her tone cool. "I'm not afraid. I just don't see the point in dredging up… whatever the lake thinks I should face."

Kian tilted his head, a faint smile tugging at his lips. "You sound awfully defensive for someone who's 'not afraid.'"

She scoffed, turning her back on the lake, her arms crossed tightly. "I don't expect you to understand. Not everything is worth digging into. Some of us… we have duties, responsibilities. Facing every buried feeling or doubt doesn't make us better at what we do."

"Doesn't it?" he replied, his voice thoughtful. "Because sometimes, the things we hide are the things that make us stronger once we understand them."

Lyra clenched her fists, her tone edged with frustration. "Strength is about control, Kian. It's about knowing who you are and staying focused, not getting lost in self-reflection."

He sighed, his gaze softening. "Maybe that's part of strength. But maybe real strength also means being willing to look at the parts of ourselves we're not proud of, the things we've tried to hide."

She looked down, her voice barely more than a whisper. "Some things are better left buried. Not all of us have the luxury of freedom like you do. For me, it's about discipline, about living up to expectations."

Kian stepped a little closer, his tone gentle but insistent. "And who set those expectations, Lyra? Your clan? Your mentors? Or… was it you?"

Her heart skipped a beat, the weight of his question settling over her, pressing against her carefully constructed defenses. She met his gaze, a flicker of defiance in her eyes. "It doesn't matter. Those expectations define me. They give me purpose."

He nodded slowly, his expression thoughtful. "Purpose is important. But you've given so much of yourself to this… this idea of duty and discipline that it feels like you're afraid to even consider anything outside of it."

She crossed her arms more tightly, looking away. "It's not about fear, Kian. It's about staying focused. Staying strong."

"Maybe," he said softly, "but strength isn't just about staying focused. It's about facing yourself, even the parts you'd rather ignore. That's what this lake does, right? Isn't that the whole point?"

She didn't answer, her gaze fixed on the ground as her mind churned. The lake's quiet presence pressed in on her, amplifying every doubt, every question she'd worked so hard to suppress. She could feel its invitation, the subtle pull to look into its depths and see whatever it was that lay hidden within herself.

Kian placed a hand on her shoulder, his touch light but grounding. "Lyra, what's the worst thing it could show you? What's the thing you're most afraid to face?"

She tensed under his touch, her voice tight. "That's the problem, Kian. I don't know. And I don't want to know."

He nodded, his gaze filled with understanding. "You're right; I don't know what it's like to live with such strict discipline, such high expectations. But I do know that not facing the truth can be even harder in the long run."

She exhaled, her shoulders slumping slightly. "What if… what if the truth is that I'm not as strong as I think? What if the lake shows me that… I'm not enough?"

He looked at her, his eyes warm with a mixture of empathy and admiration. "Lyra, strength isn't about perfection. It's about resilience. Facing yourself doesn't make you weaker—it makes you human. And there's nothing wrong with that."

She swallowed, the weight of his words mingling with the quiet invitation of the lake. She could feel her resolve softening, though she wasn't ready to admit it.

Kian stepped back, his voice gentle. "Look, I'm not here to push you into anything. But if you ever want to see what's in there… just know I'll be here with you. You don't have to face it alone."

She looked at him, her expression conflicted, a silent struggle flickering in her eyes. "I… I appreciate that," she murmured, barely able to acknowledge the vulnerability his words stirred within her.

Kian smiled, a warmth in his gaze that steadied her, though she still felt the tension of her own hesitations. The lake remained still, its surface calm, a silent invitation waiting, and though she wasn't ready to step forward, she found herself holding on to Kian's offer, letting it ground her against the lake's relentless pull.

Lyra stood at the edge of Mirror Lake, her arms crossed tightly, her posture rigid. The lake's surface was perfectly still, reflecting the trees and sky in pristine clarity, yet it seemed to pulse with a quiet power, as if it were alive, waiting for her. She felt the weight of it pressing on her, an insistent presence urging her to step forward, to see herself as she had never dared.

Kian watched her, his expression gentle yet encouraging. "You know," he said softly, "sometimes the things we fear the most are the things that have the most to teach us."

She scoffed, her gaze remaining fixed on the lake. "Easy for you to say. You seem to enjoy diving into every emotion, every thought. I prefer control."

He nodded, his voice calm. "Control has its place. But maybe this is one of those times when you could let it slip, just for a moment. Just to see what's there."

She hesitated, her pulse quickening. Every instinct urged her to step back, to leave whatever the lake held hidden beneath its surface. But Kian's steady gaze, combined with the lake's silent pull, stirred something in her, a curiosity that she couldn't quite suppress.

With a slow, steadying breath, she took a step closer, her reflection beginning to take form on the lake's mirror-like surface. For a moment, she saw herself as she expected: her stance poised and controlled, her face set in the familiar expression of discipline and focus she wore like armor.

But as she looked closer, her reflection began to shift.

The edges of her image softened, the tension in her expression easing as her reflection changed into someone else—someone both familiar and foreign. She saw herself, but with a gentleness she hadn't allowed herself in years. Her shoulders were relaxed, her gaze less guarded. There was an openness in her eyes, a quiet warmth that felt strangely unsettling, as though the lake were showing her a version of herself unbound by the rigidity she clung to.

Her breath caught, a sense of discomfort rising within her as she took in the reflection. It was her face, her figure, but with a different energy—a sense of freedom and vulnerability that she wasn't sure she wanted to acknowledge.

"What… what is this?" she whispered, her voice barely audible.

Kian took a step closer, studying her reflection as well. "It's you," he said simply. "Maybe the you that you've kept hidden."

She shook her head, her voice edged with disbelief. "This isn't me. I don't look like that."

"Maybe not on the outside," he replied gently, "but maybe it's a part of you. A part you've never let yourself see."

Lyra's gaze hardened, her tone defensive. "I don't have time for softness. Or vulnerability. That's not who I am."

Kian sighed, though his expression remained understanding. "And maybe that's why this part of you feels so foreign. Because you've pushed it down, hidden it under duty and discipline."

She turned away from the reflection, her fists clenched, her jaw tight. "I can't afford to be like that. People depend on me. Strength is all that matters."

"Strength comes in many forms, Lyra," he said softly, his gaze steady on her. "This… softer version of you doesn't make you weaker. It just makes you whole."

She swallowed, the words sinking into her, though she resisted their truth. The reflection remained calm and open, as if it were patiently waiting for her acceptance. But she could feel the tension rising within her, a silent conflict between the part of her that wanted to remain unyielding and the part of her that was curious, that yearned for the freedom her reflection seemed to embody.

She took a shaky breath, forcing herself to look back at the lake. The reflection's gentle gaze met hers, mirroring her inner struggle, and for a moment, she felt the faintest flicker of understanding—a quiet realization that perhaps strength and softness didn't have to be opposites. But as quickly as the thought came, she pushed it away, tightening her grip on her resolve.

"Maybe you're right," she said finally, her tone measured, though her voice wavered. "But I don't know if I can be that person."

Kian nodded, a gentle smile crossing his face. "Maybe you don't have to decide now. Maybe just knowing it's there is enough for now."

She glanced at him, a hint of gratitude in her eyes. "Maybe."

As she turned away from the lake, her reflection lingered in her mind, a quiet reminder of the possibilities she'd yet to embrace. And though she wasn't ready to face them fully, she couldn't deny that the lake had shown her something she couldn't forget—a version of herself with less armor, less restraint, a version she might one day choose to let in.

Lyra stepped back from the lake, her heart pounding, her mind swirling with the image she'd just seen. That reflection—softer, freer, someone she barely recognized—had shaken her more than she wanted to admit. Her fists clenched at her sides as she fought to regain her composure, every instinct screaming to push away the vulnerability that had seeped into her heart.

Kian watched her closely, a quiet understanding in his eyes. "Lyra…" he began softly.

She turned on him, her voice sharper than she intended. "Don't. Don't start with your endless lectures about 'embracing' myself or whatever nonsense you think I need to hear."

He raised his hands, his expression calm, unbothered by her outburst. "I wasn't going to lecture you. I just… wanted to make sure you're all right."

"Why wouldn't I be?" She forced a scoff, though the tension in her voice betrayed her. "It's just a lake. Some... magic trick. Nothing more."

Kian gave her a look, one that was equal parts gentle and challenging. "If it were just a trick, you wouldn't be this worked up."

Her gaze hardened, and she crossed her arms defensively. "I'm not worked up. I'm just irritated that you dragged me into this."

"Dragged you?" He tilted his head, the hint of a smile tugging at the corners of his mouth. "You were the one who walked up to the lake."

Lyra bristled, unable to shake the frustration roiling within her. "I only looked because you wouldn't stop insisting that I needed to 'confront' myself or whatever it is you think I should be doing."

He watched her for a moment, his gaze steady, refusing to rise to her bait. "Lyra, no one's saying you have to change. But maybe there's value in seeing yourself fully. Even the parts you keep hidden."

She shook her head, her voice tight. "I don't need that. I don't need... whatever this lake is showing me. It's pointless."

"Is it?" he asked quietly. "Or is it just uncomfortable?"

Her jaw clenched, the truth of his words hitting too close to the guarded places in her heart. She struggled to maintain her usual calm, to dismiss his questions, but the reflection she'd seen in the lake lingered in her mind, refusing to be ignored. "It's not real," she said finally, her voice almost a whisper. "That person isn't me."

Kian took a step closer, his tone soft but firm. "Just because it's a side you haven't let yourself acknowledge doesn't make it any less real. Vulnerability doesn't mean weakness, Lyra. Sometimes, it takes more strength to allow yourself to feel."

She looked away, her throat tight, unwilling to let him see the way his words affected her. "I don't need to feel anything. Feeling... it clouds judgment. It weakens resolve."

"Or maybe it strengthens it," he replied, his voice gentle. "Maybe being whole—embracing all parts of yourself—makes you stronger than you've ever let yourself be."

She exhaled sharply, forcing herself to brush off his words. "Strength is about control. I've spent my life training for this, Kian. Discipline, focus. Those are the things that matter."

He nodded, though his expression held a quiet understanding that unsettled her. "Those things matter, yes. But they're not all that matters. And from what I saw... there's a part of you that knows that."

Lyra's fists clenched, the flicker of truth in his words stirring something raw inside her. She straightened, her voice cold as she tried to reassert her control. "I don't need your insight, Kian. You don't understand what it takes to stay strong. To be... unbreakable."

He smiled softly, a hint of sadness in his eyes. "Maybe being unbreakable isn't the goal, Lyra. Maybe letting yourself bend, letting yourself be human, is where true strength lies."

She felt her defenses waver, her resolve slipping under the weight of his words, but she forced herself to hold firm, the echoes of her reflection haunting her thoughts. "You have no idea what you're talking about."

Kian's gaze held steady, unwavering. "Maybe not. But I see you, Lyra. All of you. And I think there's more strength in you than you've allowed yourself to believe."

She turned away, swallowing hard, unwilling to acknowledge the emotions clawing at her from within. "I don't need anyone to 'see' me," she said, though her voice lacked its usual sharpness. "I'm fine as I am."

He didn't respond, simply standing beside her, his presence a quiet, grounding force in the stillness that surrounded them. The lake's reflection faded in the darkening twilight, but the image of herself—softer, less restrained—remained imprinted in her mind.

As they walked away from the lake, Lyra kept her gaze fixed forward, her pace quick and determined, though her heart felt anything but steady. And though she wouldn't admit it, Kian's words, and the lake's silent revelation, had left a mark she couldn't quite shake.

Chapter 8
Fighting the Flame

The morning sun broke through the trees, casting faint, golden rays over the forest path. Lyra's footsteps were steady, purposeful, each step deliberate as she forced herself to focus on the task ahead. Her mind, however, felt anything but focused. The image of her reflection at Mirror Lake lingered, unbidden, haunting her with its softer edges and unguarded expression. The version of herself she'd seen there was someone she didn't recognize—and didn't want to.

She took a deep breath, steeling herself, forcing those thoughts away. She didn't need distractions. She needed clarity, focus. She'd spent years training, honing her mind and body to serve a single purpose, and she wasn't about to let one strange encounter undo her.

Just then, she heard footsteps behind her, quick and light. She didn't need to look back to know it was Kian.

"Lyra, wait up!" he called, his tone too easygoing, too familiar. It grated against the resolve she was trying to summon.

She didn't slow, didn't turn. "We have a mission, Kian. Keep your pace or fall behind."

He caught up easily, falling into stride beside her, an amused smile tugging at his lips. "Is that your way of saying 'good morning'? Because if it is, I have to say, it's a bit lacking."

Her jaw tightened, her gaze fixed forward. "I'm not here for small talk. We're here to get to the heart of this forest, complete our mission, and leave. That's all."

Kian chuckled, his tone light but probing. "Ah, so we're back to the no-nonsense soldier routine. I see."

"It's not a routine," she replied sharply, barely glancing his way. "It's who I am. And it's time you understood that."

He raised an eyebrow, his expression calm, unbothered by her coldness. "Funny, because after yesterday, I'd say there's a lot more to you than just duty and discipline."

She stiffened, but her steps didn't falter. "Yesterday was… irrelevant. It was just the forest playing tricks."

"Was it?" He tilted his head, watching her with that disarming gaze that seemed to see straight through her defenses. "Or was it you seeing a part of yourself that you've buried?"

Lyra shot him a glare, her voice sharp. "Stop. I'm done with this conversation."

Kian's gaze softened, his voice gentle. "Why? Because it makes you uncomfortable? Because it threatens the walls you've built around yourself?"

She looked away, a flash of irritation mingling with something more vulnerable. "I don't need to explain myself to you, Kian. We're not friends, and I don't need you psychoanalyzing me."

He sighed, a faint smile still tugging at his lips, though his eyes held an understanding that only deepened her irritation. "You're right; we're not friends. But that doesn't mean I don't see what's going on. You're trying to shut me out because letting someone in feels… dangerous."

She stopped abruptly, turning to face him, her expression hard. "I don't have time for 'letting people in.' I'm here for a mission, nothing more."

Kian held her gaze, his voice soft but unyielding. "But missions end, Lyra. And when they do, you'll still have yourself to face."

She scoffed, dismissing his words. "Maybe you need constant reassurance and emotional exploration, but I don't. Discipline is my strength. Focus is what keeps me going."

He studied her, his gaze unwavering. "But is it really strength if it's just a wall to keep everyone out? Even yourself?"

Her fists clenched, and she took a step back, fighting the urge to lash out further. "You have no idea what you're talking about."

Kian nodded, his expression softening. "Maybe I don't understand everything. But I do understand that shutting yourself off isn't strength, Lyra. It's isolation."

She turned away from him, trying to ignore the knot in her chest, the whisper of doubt his words stirred. "You don't understand. People rely on me. I can't afford to be… distracted."

"Maybe not," he replied gently. "But that doesn't mean you have to carry everything alone. You're not a machine, Lyra. You're human. And that means sometimes you need people, whether you like it or not."

She took a deep breath, steadying herself, forcing herself to regain her composure. "This is pointless. The sooner we complete this mission, the sooner we can part ways."

Kian's eyes held a quiet sadness, though he didn't push further. "If that's what you want."

She didn't answer, her gaze fixed forward, each step firm, disciplined. But even as she resumed her pace, she couldn't shake the lingering weight of his words, nor the unsettling realization that perhaps, deep down, a part of her wished she could believe him.

Lyra moved swiftly, her pace quicker than usual as if she could outrun the thoughts swirling in her mind. The path was narrow, winding between towering trees, but she kept her focus forward, each step precise, calculated. She could feel Kian's presence behind her, his footsteps light as he trailed after her, unbothered by her brisk pace. She'd hoped he would take the hint and leave her to her thoughts, but within moments, he'd caught up, falling into step beside her with that familiar, infuriating ease.

"Trying to outrun something?" he asked, his tone casual, a hint of amusement in his voice. "Or just determined to leave me in the dust?"

She didn't break her stride, her gaze fixed ahead. "I don't remember inviting you to join me."

Kian chuckled, unfazed. "You don't need to invite me. Besides, I'd hate for you to get too far ahead. Who knows what trouble you might get into without me?"

Lyra shot him a sidelong glare, her voice clipped. "I don't need anyone's help, least of all yours."

He raised an eyebrow, a playful smile on his face. "So defensive, as always. You know, you don't have to be so guarded all the time."

She scoffed, dismissing his words. "It's called caution, Kian. Something you clearly know nothing about."

He sighed, shaking his head. "Caution is one thing. But keeping everyone at arm's length? That's something else entirely."

She felt a flicker of annoyance rise within her, mingling with the uneasy memories of Mirror Lake. That reflection—softer, more open—hovered in her mind, an image she couldn't quite banish. "Maybe you enjoy sharing every stray thought and feeling, but I don't. Some of us value restraint."

Kian's gaze softened, though his voice remained light. "Maybe restraint isn't the only way to be strong, Lyra. Maybe there's strength in letting people in, even if just a little."

She clenched her jaw, refusing to let his words sink in. "I don't need to 'let people in.' I'm fine as I am. Focused."

He nodded slowly, though his eyes held a hint of sadness. "If you say so. But I wonder… is it really focus, or just fear of what you might find if you let those walls down?"

Her steps faltered slightly, the question hitting closer than she wanted to admit. The reflection from the lake seemed to flicker at the edge of her mind, that image of herself unguarded, unburdened. She'd spent years perfecting her discipline, shaping herself into someone defined by purpose and control. But that version of herself—soft, unshielded—had unsettled her in a way she couldn't shake.

"What I might find doesn't matter," she replied, her tone colder than she intended. "What matters is getting the job done. Duty comes first."

Kian glanced at her, his expression thoughtful. "And what about after? When the mission's over, and you're left with only yourself?"

She looked away, unwilling to meet his gaze, her voice steady but hollow. "Then I'll still have my purpose. That's more than enough."

For a moment, he said nothing, merely walking beside her, his presence a quiet contrast to the steady rhythm of her footsteps. She could feel his gaze on her, unassuming yet perceptive, as though he could see the conflict she was trying so hard to bury.

Finally, he spoke, his voice gentle. "I think there's more to you than purpose and duty, Lyra. And maybe, one day, you'll let yourself see that, too."

She didn't answer, her silence heavy as she kept her gaze forward, pushing down the whisper of doubt that lingered in her mind. But as they walked, the memory of her reflection remained, a reminder of a self she couldn't quite ignore.

The forest grew darker as Lyra and Kian moved deeper into its heart. Shadows stretched across the path, their forms twisting and shifting in the dim light, and the air grew thick with the unmistakable sense of something lurking nearby. Lyra's senses sharpened, her every instinct on high alert. She scanned the trees, her hand instinctively tightening on the hilt of her blade.

Beside her, Kian walked with an unhurried ease, though she could tell by the way his hand hovered near his weapon that he, too, was prepared for anything. The silence between them was filled with an unspoken tension, the earlier conversation hanging heavy in the air. Lyra pushed it from her mind, focusing on her surroundings, reminding herself of her mission and purpose.

But then, without warning, the shadows around them came alive.

A low growl sounded from the trees, and suddenly, dark, wiry creatures emerged from the underbrush, their eyes glinting with a feral hunger. They were swift and silent, their movements calculated, as though they'd been waiting for the perfect moment to strike.

Lyra drew her blade, stepping forward, her posture tense and ready. "Stay close," she murmured, not looking at Kian. "These things move fast."

He nodded, his gaze narrowing as he summoned a small flame in his palm, the flickering light illuminating his face. "I'll take the ones on the right. Try to keep up."

She shot him a sidelong glare. "I can handle myself."

Kian merely smirked, his focus shifting to the approaching creatures. With a quick, fluid motion, he extended his arm, sending a wave of fire across the ground in front of them. The creatures recoiled, momentarily thrown off by the sudden burst of light and heat, but they quickly regrouped, lunging forward with renewed ferocity.

Lyra moved in sync with Kian, her blade slicing through the air as she deflected one of the creatures' attacks. She felt the heat of Kian's flames beside her, bright and fierce, and she found herself instinctively moving closer, using the glow to guide her strikes, to ground herself in the chaos.

The creatures circled them, relentless, their movements coordinated as they tried to break through the barrier of flame and steel. Lyra gritted her teeth, each strike precise, every motion a testament to her discipline. But for every creature she cut down, another took its place, their dark forms blending with the shadows, their attacks swift and relentless.

Kian's fire flared brighter, pushing back the creatures with each wave of heat. Lyra could feel the intensity of his power beside her, the flames casting long shadows across the forest floor, and she realized, with a flicker of discomfort, that she was beginning to rely on his fire to keep the creatures at bay. The thought unsettled her, but there was no time to dwell on it as another creature lunged at her from the side.

"Kian!" she called out instinctively, her voice sharper than intended.

He reacted instantly, sending a burst of flame in her direction, the creature recoiling with a shriek as the fire consumed it. Lyra took the opening, striking down another creature that had tried to flank her. As she regained her footing, she cast a quick glance at Kian, who was watching her with a mixture of concern and something else—a flicker of something unspoken that made her pulse quicken.

"You're welcome," he said, a hint of teasing in his voice, though his eyes held a seriousness that belied his tone.

She bristled, frustrated with herself for needing his help. "I had it under control."

"Sure you did," he replied smoothly, sending another wave of flame toward the creatures. "You know, you could just admit you're glad I'm here."

She clenched her jaw, her focus returning to the fight as she struck down another creature. "Don't flatter yourself. I don't rely on anyone."

"Right," he said, his tone light but with an edge of sincerity. "And yet, here we are, fighting side by side. Feels like teamwork to me."

Lyra forced herself to ignore him, but she couldn't deny the truth in his words. The creatures were relentless, their movements erratic, and every time she thought she'd gained control, another attacked from a new angle, forcing her to rely on Kian's flames to hold them off. The fire created a barrier, a circle of protection that allowed her to focus her strikes more effectively, and as much as she hated to admit it, she was grateful for it.

The battle wore on, the creatures finally beginning to thin as they struck them down one by one. But even as the threat diminished, Lyra's frustration grew, a tight knot in her chest. She was used to fighting alone, to relying solely on her own strength and skill. But now, here she was, depending on Kian's flames, his presence beside her a stabilizing force she hadn't realized she needed.

With a final, powerful strike, she dispatched the last creature, and the forest fell silent once more, the only sounds their ragged breathing and the crackling of Kian's flames as they dimmed.

He looked at her, his gaze steady. "You all right?"

Lyra straightened, sheathing her blade, her voice clipped. "I'm fine. This… it was nothing."

Kian studied her, a knowing look in his eyes. "You know, it's okay to admit that working together made things easier."

She bristled, her defenses flaring. "I didn't need your help."

He shrugged, an easy smile tugging at his lips. "Maybe not. But you used it anyway."

She turned away, unwilling to let him see the flicker of conflict in her eyes. "This doesn't change anything. I still work alone."

"Sure," he replied, though his tone held a warmth that was impossible to ignore. "Whatever you say, Lyra."

As they resumed their path, Lyra couldn't shake the feeling of frustration and confusion that lingered. The lake's reflection, the creatures, her reliance on Kian's fire—it all seemed to blur together, challenging everything she'd held as true. But she forced herself to push it down, to focus on the path ahead, even as the questions remained, gnawing at the edges of her mind.

The forest was quiet again as they walked, the creatures defeated and the shadows retreating into the trees. The path ahead was winding, the ground scattered with fallen leaves, and the light filtering through the branches had softened, creating a momentary sense of calm. But Lyra's mind was anything but calm.

The fight had left her unsettled, not because of the danger, but because of how naturally she had fallen into step with Kian. She hated that she had depended on his flames, that she had let herself rely on someone else, even for a moment. She glanced at him, hoping he wouldn't notice the tension in her gaze, but he seemed to have other plans.

"So," Kian said, breaking the silence, "are you ever going to admit it?"

She shot him a wary look, her voice clipped. "Admit what?"

He chuckled, shaking his head. "That you're the most stubborn person I've ever met."

She huffed, her tone dismissive. "I don't see what my 'stubbornness,' as you call it, has to do with anything."

He raised an eyebrow, his smile easy yet probing. "Really? Because it seems to me like you'd rather bite off your own tongue than say you're glad I was there in that fight."

Lyra rolled her eyes, her steps brisk as she tried to ignore him. "I don't need to justify my actions to you, Kian. We fought together. That's it."

He smirked, his gaze steady on her. "But that's not it, is it? You can't even admit that you might have trusted me, even just a little."

She stiffened, her voice taut with irritation. "Trusting someone in the middle of a fight is not the same as trusting them personally. Don't mistake necessity for something it's not."

Kian chuckled, his tone both amused and challenging. "You keep telling yourself that. But I think there's more to it. You don't want to admit that relying on someone else might actually make you stronger."

Her gaze flashed with defiance. "I don't need anyone else to be strong. I've trained my whole life to handle things alone."

"Ah," he said, his voice softening. "But what if strength isn't just about handling everything alone?"

She clenched her jaw, unwilling to let his words reach the part of her that was already questioning. "That's the only strength I need. If I relied on others every time things got difficult, I'd be weak."

He stopped, turning to face her fully, his gaze intense. "Or maybe, Lyra, trusting someone isn't a weakness at all. Maybe it's another kind of strength."

She glared at him, her voice edged with defensiveness. "You don't understand. People rely on me. I don't have the luxury of depending on others. That's not how I was raised."

Kian tilted his head, his eyes searching her face, soft yet unyielding. "I get it. You're carrying a lot on your shoulders. But have you ever thought that letting someone share the weight doesn't make you any less capable?"

Her fists clenched at her sides, his words stirring an inner conflict she wasn't prepared to face. "Duty isn't about sharing burdens. It's about being strong enough to carry them alone."

"Is it?" he challenged gently, his voice laced with empathy. "Or is that just what you've been taught to believe?"

She turned away, her gaze fixed on the trees ahead, her voice hollow. "It's what keeps me focused. What keeps me… strong."

Kian let out a soft sigh, and when he spoke again, his tone was free of its usual teasing, his words calm but piercing. "Lyra, I don't think being strong means shutting everyone out. I think it's being willing to let someone in, even when it's hard."

She didn't respond, her silence heavy with unspoken doubts and questions. The image of her reflection at Mirror Lake, that unguarded version of herself, flickered in her mind, challenging everything she thought she knew about strength, discipline, and trust.

After a moment, he spoke again, his voice gentle. "I can see it, you know. The way you struggle with this. The way you want to keep pushing everyone away, but you're curious too. About what it might mean to… trust."

Her voice was barely more than a whisper. "Curiosity is dangerous. It leads to distraction."

Kian smiled, his tone soft. "Or it leads to growth. You don't have to change everything about yourself, Lyra. But maybe letting someone in doesn't have to change who you are. Maybe it just adds to it."

She looked at him, her expression conflicted, a quiet vulnerability slipping through her guarded facade. "You're making this sound simple. It's not."

He nodded, his gaze steady. "I know. But sometimes, the hardest things are the ones worth considering."

She looked away, her resolve wavering as her mind swirled with the tension between duty and the growing curiosity she couldn't ignore. "This mission is what matters. Nothing else."

Kian didn't push further, his voice calm as he replied. "Then we'll focus on the mission. But just know, Lyra... I'm here, whether you choose to let me in or not."

They walked in silence after that, the unspoken words lingering between them, a quiet reminder of the questions she wasn't yet ready to answer. And as they moved forward, Lyra couldn't shake the feeling that the walls she had built were no longer as solid as they once seemed, the pull of curiosity slowly chipping away at her resolve.

Chapter 9
Between Shadows and Light

The forest had taken on a different quality since they'd left Mirror Lake. It was subtle, a barely-there hum beneath the surface of everything, but Lyra could feel it—an awareness that seemed to follow her every step. It was as if the lake's magic had seeped into the very air, heightening everything, bringing her emotions to the forefront, refusing to let them fade. And though she tried to ignore it, she could feel the effect pulling her attention to Kian in ways she wasn't prepared for.

They walked side by side, the silence between them heavy yet charged. Lyra's focus, usually sharp and unyielding, kept drifting, her thoughts looping back to the moments they'd shared, the reflections in the lake, and his words, which lingered longer than they should have. She stole a glance at him, watching the way he moved with ease, his eyes alert yet somehow softened in the forest's quiet. He met her gaze, his lips curving in a faint, knowing smile.

"You're unusually quiet," he remarked, his voice breaking the silence, warm and gentle. "Thinking about anything in particular?"

Lyra looked away, her pulse quickening, and forced a dismissive tone. "No. Just focused on the path ahead."

"Focused?" he echoed with a smirk. "Or maybe still thinking about what we saw back there?"

She bristled, hoping he couldn't see the way his words affected her. "There's nothing to think about. It was… just a moment."

"Just a moment?" Kian chuckled, his tone light but probing. "Interesting. Because it seemed to me like it was a bit more than that."

Lyra felt a flicker of irritation, though she wasn't sure if it was directed at him or herself. "You're reading too much into things, Kian. Not everything has to be analyzed."

He shrugged, his gaze drifting over the trees before landing back on her. "Maybe. But I don't think you'd be this rattled if it didn't mean something."

She frowned, her voice defensive. "I'm not rattled. I'm just… cautious. There's a difference."

"Of course," he replied smoothly, though his eyes held a glint of amusement. "Cautious. Nothing more."

They continued in silence for a moment, but Lyra could feel the tension between them, the unspoken words hanging in the air. She wanted to brush it off, to dismiss whatever strange effect the lake had had on her, but it lingered, its presence growing with each step. She felt drawn to Kian in a way that made her heart beat faster, and the awareness unsettled her.

Kian glanced at her, his tone softening. "Lyra… you don't always have to be so guarded. You know that, right?"

She shot him a quick look, her tone sharp. "Guardedness is what keeps people safe. It's what keeps me strong."

He nodded, thoughtful. "But does it also keep you… alone?"

She didn't answer, his question striking closer than she wanted to admit. The lake's effect seemed to press in on her, amplifying everything she'd been trying to ignore. For the first time, she allowed herself to consider that maybe, just maybe, she was more drawn to Kian than she'd let herself believe.

Finally, after a long pause, she spoke, her voice quieter. "What do you want from me, Kian?"

He stopped, turning to face her fully, his expression open, unguarded. "I don't want anything from you, Lyra. I just… I want you to let yourself be."

She looked at him, feeling a warmth in his gaze that made her stomach flip. "I don't know how to do that."

He smiled, a gentle understanding in his eyes. "Maybe you don't have to know. Maybe you just have to let it happen."

Lyra swallowed, her gaze dropping to the ground. The part of her that clung to discipline and duty resisted his words, but another part—a part that felt closer to the version of herself she'd seen in the lake—wanted to listen, to let herself feel without questioning.

When she looked up, Kian's expression was soft, his eyes filled with a quiet encouragement. "We don't always have to fight everything, Lyra. Sometimes… we just have to let things be."

She nodded slowly, her defenses slipping, even if just for a moment. And as they resumed their walk, the tension between them remained, but it was different now—a quiet, unspoken understanding that neither of them seemed in a hurry to break.

As they walked deeper into the forest, the tension from Mirror Lake softened, replaced by a quieter, more reflective air. The path was winding and dense with shadows, but there was a sense of calm, as if the forest itself had paused, waiting for something unspoken to pass between them.

Kian broke the silence first, his tone lighter than usual but laced with something that made Lyra glance over, curiosity stirring. "You know," he began, "there are things I'm afraid of too."

Lyra's brow furrowed, surprised by his admission. "Afraid? You?" She tried to keep her tone neutral, but there was a flicker of interest she couldn't hide. "I thought you were the fearless one."

He chuckled softly, though his gaze remained serious. "Fearless, huh? I'm far from that." He paused, then glanced at her, his face open in a way she wasn't used to. "If I seem that way, maybe it's because I'm better at hiding it."

She looked at him, her curiosity deepening. "Hiding what exactly?"

Kian hesitated, a hint of vulnerability slipping through his usual confidence. "Freedom... it's everything to me. My clan, we believe in it so deeply that it's a part of who we are. But sometimes... sometimes, I wonder if I'll ever find a place that truly feels like home."

Lyra blinked, taken aback. This was a side of Kian she hadn't seen before—one that was open, unguarded, and unmistakably human. "A place that feels like home?"

He nodded, his gaze distant. "For all our talk of freedom, sometimes it feels like I'm just... drifting. Moving from place to place, never really belonging anywhere."

There was a softness in his voice, a quiet sincerity that resonated with something within her. She tried to ignore the feeling, tried to brush it off, but his words lingered, pressing on her own defenses. "I never would have guessed," she murmured, her voice almost gentle. "You always seem so... sure of yourself."

Kian smiled, though there was a sadness in his eyes. "Everyone has their doubts, Lyra. Even those of us who seem like we're always on solid ground."

Lyra looked away, trying to quell the softness creeping into her voice. "So, all this talk of freedom... it's not enough for you?"

"It is," he replied quietly, his gaze steady. "But it comes with its own kind of loneliness. The idea that maybe… maybe I'll always be searching, but never finding."

The words hung between them, thick with unspoken meaning. Lyra felt something shift within her, a flicker of understanding she hadn't expected. She wanted to brush it off, to turn away, but there was something in his vulnerability that stirred a response she couldn't quite suppress.

"Maybe that's just… life," she said finally, her voice softer than usual. "Maybe we're all just searching for something, even if we don't know what it is."

Kian looked at her, a hint of surprise in his eyes. "Didn't think you were one for philosophical thoughts."

She shrugged, an almost shy smile slipping through her usual guarded expression. "I'm not. But… I understand what it's like to feel like you're always striving for something. Something that's just out of reach."

He nodded slowly, his gaze warm. "I suppose that's the thing that binds us, then. Different paths, but maybe… the same kind of struggle."

Lyra tried to mask the tenderness that crept into her expression, forcing herself to keep her tone steady. "Struggle is part of life. It's what makes us strong."

Kian smiled, his eyes softening as he looked at her. "And maybe it's what makes us human, too. All of us carrying around these hidden fears, these things we don't let anyone see."

She held his gaze, a strange warmth blossoming in her chest. "Maybe."

They walked in silence for a moment, and Lyra could feel her guard slipping, bit by bit. For the first time, she saw Kian not as the lighthearted wanderer he so often portrayed, but as someone with his own fears and doubts. It made him feel… closer, somehow, like an ally in the unspoken battles they both fought.

After a pause, she murmured, "Thank you for sharing that. I… I didn't expect it."

Kian's smile was gentle, almost relieved. "I suppose it's easier to share when you're with someone who understands."

Lyra looked away, fighting the small smile that threatened to appear. "Maybe," she said softly. And as they continued forward, she couldn't shake the feeling that the lake's influence had given her more than just a glimpse of herself—it had allowed her to see Kian, truly, for the first time.

They had stopped to rest by a small, clear stream that trickled through the forest, its surface calm and glassy. The sunlight filtered through the trees, casting dappled patterns on the water. Lyra knelt by the edge, cupping her hands to take a drink, but as she leaned forward, she caught sight of her reflection in the stream's surface, and her breath caught.

She hadn't thought about Mirror Lake in hours, but now, here in the quiet of the forest, the stream's reflection held a similar magic. She could see her own face—yet it was different from the way she remembered. There was a softness around her eyes, a calmness she wasn't used to seeing, and it startled her.

Kian's voice pulled her from her thoughts. "You look deep in thought," he said, sitting beside her, a faint smile on his face. "What are you seeing?"

She hesitated, almost brushing him off, but something held her back. "I... I'm seeing myself," she said slowly, her voice barely above a whisper. "But I don't recognize who I am anymore."

Kian leaned in, his gaze warm and curious. "What do you mean?"

She let out a slow breath, watching the ripples on the water as if they could answer her question. "I've always known exactly who I am. Discipline, focus, duty—that's what defines me. But now... now I'm not so sure."

Kian's eyes softened. "And what's wrong with that?"

Lyra shook her head, struggling to find the words. "It feels... unsettling. My purpose has always been clear. But meeting you, seeing my reflection—it's as if something inside me is shifting."

He looked at her with a gentle understanding, his voice calm. "Change can be unsettling, Lyra. But it doesn't have to be a bad thing."

She glanced at him, her expression conflicted. "You say that as if it's simple."

"Because maybe it is," he replied, his voice almost a whisper. "Maybe sometimes we make things more complicated than they need to be."

She sighed, a faint bitterness creeping into her tone. "My life has never been simple, Kian. Duty, discipline… it's what keeps me grounded. If I let myself change… if I let myself feel…"

"Then maybe you'll find a new kind of strength," he said softly, his gaze never wavering. "A strength that doesn't come from shutting everything out but from letting yourself in."

She looked down, her fingers tracing patterns in the dirt beside the stream. "But if I change, if I let go of the things that define me, then who am I?"

Kian's smile was gentle, understanding. "Maybe that's exactly what you need to discover."

Lyra closed her eyes, her voice barely more than a murmur. "I don't know how to do that. I don't know if I want to."

Kian reached out, his hand brushing lightly against hers, grounding her. "You don't have to know everything right now,

Lyra. This journey isn't about having all the answers—it's about finding them along the way."

She opened her eyes, looking at him with a vulnerability she rarely allowed herself to show. "I've spent my whole life pushing down what I feel. What if… what if I'm just weak without it?"

He shook his head, his gaze steady. "You're not weak. You're brave. Brave enough to question, to face yourself, even if it scares you."

Her hand hovered near his, the warmth of his touch lingering, pulling her back to the reflection in the stream. She saw herself there again, the softness around her eyes, the flicker of something undefinable but real. "I never thought I could be someone different," she whispered, her voice laced with wonder and fear. "But… I think I am."

Kian squeezed her hand gently. "Then maybe it's time to let that part of you grow. To let yourself be more than just duty and discipline."

Lyra felt a lump rise in her throat, a mix of fear and hope entwined. She looked at him, her voice fragile yet determined. "But what if this part of me isn't enough? What if… I lose my purpose?"

Kian's eyes held a quiet reassurance, a warmth that seemed to reach the parts of her she'd kept hidden. "Purpose isn't something you lose, Lyra. It's something you discover, again and again. Maybe this change isn't taking anything from you—it's giving you a chance to be more."

She looked back at the stream, her reflection staring up at her, and for the first time, she allowed herself to truly see it. The softness, the openness, the vulnerability—it wasn't weakness. It was simply a different kind of strength, one she hadn't allowed herself to feel before.

With a shaky breath, she nodded, barely acknowledging the small, silent decision she'd made. "Maybe you're right," she said softly. "Maybe there's more to me than I've allowed."

Kian's smile widened, a hint of pride in his eyes. "That's all I've ever wanted you to see."

As they sat by the stream, the forest around them quiet and watchful, Lyra felt something shift within her, a subtle yet undeniable change. And though part of her was still afraid, she knew that this was a beginning—a new path, one she hadn't planned for but was finally willing to explore.

Lyra rose from the edge of the stream, her mind swirling with the echo of Kian's words and the reflection she'd seen staring back at her. It was her own face—yet layered with something unfamiliar, something softer and less guarded. She couldn't shake the feeling that, in some inexplicable way, this part of her had been awakened because of him.

But as she brushed off her hands and steadied her breathing, the weight of her purpose settled over her once more. She had a mission. A clear, unwavering duty that she'd been raised to uphold. It was what gave her life structure and direction, the thing she could rely on when everything else was uncertain.

Duty first, she reminded herself, her resolve hardening.

Kian had fallen a few steps behind, allowing her a moment of solitude. She was grateful for it—his presence was becoming a distraction, an ever-present tug at the edges of her thoughts. He was like a flame she was drawn to but knew could burn her. He represented a freedom and openness that threatened to unravel the very discipline she had built her life around.

Yet, as she walked, she felt his warmth behind her, his silent support both comforting and deeply unsettling. His words echoed in her mind, each one gently prying at the walls she'd worked so hard to keep intact. *Strength doesn't always mean shutting people out. Sometimes, it means letting them in.*

Lyra gritted her teeth, quickening her pace. She needed distance, needed to focus. Allowing her emotions to cloud her judgment could jeopardize everything she'd worked for. Her thoughts sharpened as she forced herself to visualize the mission's end, the success that lay ahead, the sense of completion and pride she would feel when she could return to her clan having done what she set out to do.

But no matter how hard she tried to push Kian from her mind, his presence lingered, tugging at the parts of her she didn't want to acknowledge.

He spoke up quietly behind her. "You're awfully quiet."

She didn't turn, keeping her voice steady. "There's nothing to talk about. We have a mission to complete."

He fell into step beside her, studying her with that same steady, disarming gaze. "I get it. Duty and all. But there's more than just the mission here, Lyra. You feel it, too."

She clenched her fists, forcing herself to keep her gaze forward. "Duty is what gives my life meaning. Everything else is secondary."

Kian's expression softened, though he didn't press her further. "If that's what you believe."

The silence between them was thick, his unspoken words hanging in the air, tugging at her with a weight she wasn't ready to confront. She could feel her heart quicken, her resolve wavering as she struggled to reconcile the growing bond with Kian and her unwavering commitment to her mission.

This is just a distraction, she told herself, her inner voice stern and unyielding. *This feeling—whatever it is—will pass. It has to.*

But even as she tried to harden her heart, she couldn't shake the quiet, insistent voice in the back of her mind, whispering that maybe—just maybe—there was room for both duty and something more.

As they continued forward, her mind and heart at war, Lyra's grip on her purpose remained firm, but the certainty with which she'd held it now felt different, clouded by something she hadn't allowed herself to consider until now. And though she couldn't deny the pull she felt toward Kian, she steeled herself, determined to keep her emotions in check, to focus on what truly mattered.

But deep down, a part of her knew that the path ahead would only grow more complicated from here.

Chapter 10
Divided Loyalties

As Lyra and Kian moved deeper into the heart of the forest, the air grew thick with an unfamiliar tension. The stillness was oppressive, the usual sounds of forest life replaced by an uneasy silence. Lyra's senses sharpened, her every instinct on high alert. Her hand drifted to the hilt of her blade, fingers tightening in anticipation as she scanned the surroundings.

It was then that she spotted it—a faint mark etched into the trunk of a tree, barely noticeable against the bark, but unmistakable to anyone who knew what to look for. Her eyes narrowed as she reached out to touch the mark, her pulse quickening.

"Kian," she said, her voice low and tense.

He stopped beside her, glancing at the tree. "What is it?"

She didn't look at him, her focus fixed on the mark. "This is the symbol of the Shadowfangs," she murmured. "The rival clan."

He frowned, leaning closer. "They've been through here?"

"Recently," she replied, her tone clipped. "These marks are fresh. They're moving through the forest, maybe closer than we thought."

Kian straightened, his gaze shifting warily to their surroundings. "Then we'll have to be careful."

Lyra shot him a quick, guarded look, her voice edged with suspicion. "You don't understand, Kian. The Shadowfangs aren't just a rival clan—they're dangerous, ruthless. And they don't take kindly to intruders."

He held her gaze, a calm reassurance in his eyes. "Then we'll stay alert. But that doesn't mean we should start doubting each other now."

She scoffed, a hint of tension slipping into her tone. "Easy for you to say. You've never had to face them."

Kian's expression softened, though his eyes held a firm resolve. "I may not know them like you do, but I know how to stay cautious, Lyra. You don't have to keep reminding me."

Lyra took a step back, crossing her arms defensively. "I do if you keep acting like this is just another mission. You don't understand what they're capable of."

He tilted his head, his voice steady. "Then explain it to me. Help me understand."

Her jaw clenched, a flicker of frustration sparking in her gaze. "The Shadowfangs don't follow the same rules we do. They're... unpredictable. Ruthless. Trusting anyone outside our clan has always been a mistake when it comes to them."

Kian's brows furrowed, his voice softening. "And you think trusting me is a mistake, too?"

She hesitated, her gaze flickering as she struggled to find the right words. "It's... complicated. You're not one of them, but you're not one of us, either. And in situations like this, that matters."

He sighed, his tone gentle but insistent. "Lyra, I'm here with you. We're in this together. Isn't that enough?"

She looked away, her voice guarded. "In a perfect world, maybe. But I can't afford to take risks. Not when the Shadowfangs are involved."

"So what?" he replied, his tone a little sharper. "You're just going to shut me out? After everything we've been through?"

Her gaze hardened, her voice dropping. "This isn't about what we've been through. This is about survival, Kian. If you're not careful, if you're not prepared... they'll use that against you."

He stepped closer, his expression resolute. "I get it, Lyra. You're used to relying on yourself, and maybe you don't trust easily. But pushing me away won't keep us safe. If anything, it'll make things more dangerous."

She looked at him, a flicker of conflict in her eyes. "You don't understand. The Shadowfangs... they don't just attack. They find your weaknesses and exploit them. If they sense any division between us, they'll use it."

Kian held her gaze, his voice unwavering. "Then don't give them the satisfaction. Trust me, Lyra. Let's face them as a team."

Her jaw tightened, a silent struggle evident in her expression. She wanted to trust him, to lean on him in this moment, but her instincts—honed by years of discipline and duty—warned her against it. The Shadowfangs were ruthless, and she couldn't afford to let her guard down, not even with him.

"I… I don't know if I can do that," she murmured, her voice barely audible.

He took another step closer, his voice gentle. "You can. And you don't have to do it alone."

A long silence settled between them, heavy with unspoken doubts and fears. Lyra's gaze dropped, her fingers loosening on the hilt of her blade as she struggled to reconcile the pull she felt toward him with the ingrained wariness that had kept her safe for so long.

Finally, she took a breath, her tone soft but edged with resolve. "Fine. We'll work together. But if I sense anything—anything—that feels off, I won't hesitate to act."

Kian nodded, a faint smile playing at his lips. "Fair enough. But I don't think you'll regret it."

She didn't respond, though her expression softened just slightly as she turned her focus back to the forest. The signs of the rival clan were scattered around them, a stark reminder of the dangers that lay ahead. But as they moved forward, she felt a strange, tentative sense of trust taking root—a trust she wasn't sure she was ready for, but one that, despite her doubts, she found herself willing to explore.

The forest seemed to darken around them, the air thickening as if the very shadows were alive, watching, waiting. Lyra's senses prickled, a tension rising in the pit of her stomach. She felt the familiar weight of her blade at her side, her muscles coiled, ready. Beside her, Kian held up his hand, a flicker of flame dancing in his palm, casting a warm glow against the encroaching darkness.

"Kian," she whispered, her eyes scanning the trees around them. "They're close."

He nodded, his gaze intense. "I can feel it too."

Suddenly, from the shadows, dark forms emerged, their eyes gleaming with a predatory hunger. These were no ordinary creatures; they seemed born from the very darkness that cloaked the forest, their bodies shifting and formless, tendrils of shadow reaching toward them with a silent, sinister intent.

Lyra didn't hesitate. With a swift motion, she drew her blade, her shadows deepening and swirling around her, amplifying her power. She felt Kian step closer, his flame flaring to life beside her, its warmth mingling with the cold energy of her shadows in an unexpectedly harmonious way.

The first creature lunged at her, its form twisting and reforming mid-air. She slashed through it, her shadow-infused blade cutting through the darkness with ease. At the same moment, Kian raised his hand, a wall of fire surging forward to repel another creature attempting to flank them. The fire and shadows met, merging at the edges, creating a barrier that seemed to unnerve the creatures, forcing them to hesitate.

"Lyra, behind you!" Kian called out, his voice sharp.

She spun, her shadows reacting instantly, forming a shield that absorbed the attack of a creature that had slipped in close. She felt the impact but held steady, her blade flashing as she struck back. The creature dissipated into wisps of shadow, but more took its place, relentless and unforgiving.

Kian moved beside her, his flame dancing and shifting, complementing her every move. Their attacks seemed to flow in perfect sync, his fire igniting in the spaces her shadows left open, her shadows reinforcing the gaps in his flames. It was an intricate, unspoken dance, one that neither of them had practiced but seemed instinctively to know.

She stole a glance at him, momentarily struck by the way his power melded with hers. "How are we… doing this?"

He grinned, not missing a beat as he blasted another creature with fire. "I have no idea. Guess we just… fit."

Lyra felt a flicker of something unnameable, a sensation both thrilling and unnerving. "Don't get too comfortable," she muttered, striking down another creature, though the usual edge in her tone softened. "This doesn't change anything."

"Maybe not," he replied, his voice filled with quiet confidence. "But it feels right, doesn't it?"

She wanted to deny it, to brush him off, but as she slashed through another shadow creature, her shadows entwining seamlessly with his flames, she couldn't ignore the truth. Their powers weren't just coexisting; they were enhancing each other, creating a synergy that neither could achieve alone.

Another creature lunged at them, larger than the others, its form shifting and twisting, dark tendrils lashing out toward them both. Without thinking, Lyra moved to intercept it, her shadows wrapping around the tendrils, restraining the creature just long enough for Kian to step forward, his flame blazing with a fierce intensity as he struck. His fire and her shadows merged, a single, powerful force that overwhelmed the creature, reducing it to nothing more than a wisp of smoke that vanished into the air.

As the last of the creatures dissipated, they stood in silence, catching their breath. The forest was quiet again, but the air still hummed with the remnants of their combined energy. Lyra's gaze shifted to Kian, a question burning in her mind, one she wasn't sure she wanted to ask.

"That... that shouldn't have worked," she said, her voice barely above a whisper. "Our powers—shadow and flame—they're supposed to be opposites."

Kian met her gaze, his eyes bright with a mixture of amusement and something deeper. "Maybe they're only opposites because we believe they are."

She frowned, her mind racing. "But that's the way it's always been. Our clans… they're different. Divided."

"Are they, though?" he asked gently, stepping closer. "Or is that just a story we've been told?"

She opened her mouth to reply, but no words came. For so long, she had been taught that her clan's power was distinct, separate, and that mixing with other clans—especially those like Kian's—was forbidden, even dangerous. Yet here they were, their powers mingling as if they were two parts of a whole.

He looked at her, his expression earnest. "Lyra, what if we're stronger together?"

Her heart skipped a beat, the truth of his words resonating in a way that unsettled her. She wanted to push him away, to dismiss the thought, but she couldn't deny what she had just experienced. They had fought in perfect harmony, their strengths amplifying each other's, bridging a divide she'd thought was impossible to cross.

Finally, she managed to find her voice, though it was softer, almost vulnerable. "I don't know if I can believe that, Kian. I've spent my whole life learning that we're… separate. Different."

He reached out, his hand hovering near hers, close enough that she could feel the warmth of his presence. "Maybe that's something worth unlearning."

She looked at his hand, the unspoken offer in his gesture both terrifying and strangely comforting. The logical part of her mind resisted, reminding her of her duty, of everything she'd been taught. But another part of her—a part that was growing louder—felt the pull toward something new, something she'd never let herself consider before.

With a quiet, shaky breath, she stepped back, her gaze still locked on his. "This changes nothing. We're here for a mission."

Kian's smile was gentle, understanding, though she could see the spark of hope in his eyes. "Understood. But maybe, one day, you'll see that it doesn't have to be one or the other."

She didn't respond, her mind and heart at war as they resumed their path. But even as she tried to focus on the mission, she couldn't shake the feeling that, in that battle, she had glimpsed a truth about herself, and about Kian, that she couldn't easily ignore.

The forest was quiet again, the echoes of the recent battle fading into the thick canopy above them. Lyra sheathed her blade, glancing at the faint, smoky tendrils that lingered from the defeated shadow creatures. Despite her attempts to brush off the connection she felt with Kian, the way they'd fought together was undeniable—a perfect, instinctive partnership. As she dusted off her hands and steadied her breathing, her mind swirled with conflicting thoughts.

Kian moved beside her, his gaze lingering on her with a quiet, unspoken understanding. She felt his eyes on her, a steady warmth that seemed to reach through her guarded exterior, and she turned slightly, keeping her tone even. "We should keep moving."

He nodded, though he didn't look away. "Agreed. But you look like there's something on your mind."

She stiffened, a flash of annoyance sparking within her. "Nothing that concerns you."

Kian tilted his head, his eyes gentle but knowing. "You don't have to hide it, Lyra. I know what this must be like for you—trusting someone from outside your clan, relying on our powers together. It's… a lot to take in."

She looked away, her gaze fixed on the path ahead, the leaves crunching under her boots. "It's not just a lot, Kian. It's forbidden. Everything about this… partnership… goes against what I've been taught."

He fell silent, his expression thoughtful. "But does that mean it's wrong?"

She clenched her fists, the internal battle raging within her. "According to my clan, it does. We're raised to believe that alliances with outsiders lead to weakness, to compromise. And what we just did—fighting side by side, our powers blending like that—it's something I've never been allowed to consider."

Kian sighed, glancing at her with a mixture of empathy and frustration. "You're following rules that were made long before either of us were even born. Maybe they don't have to define you."

Lyra hesitated, feeling the weight of his words settle over her. "It's not that simple. Those rules are there for a reason. They protect us. My clan… we rely on discipline, on tradition. Without it, we risk everything."

He placed a hand on her shoulder, his touch grounding. "I understand tradition. But Lyra, you've just proven that there's strength in breaking that tradition. When we fought together, we were stronger than either of us would've been alone. Doesn't that mean something?"

She shook his hand off, her voice sharper than intended. "Maybe it does. But if my clan finds out, if they even suspect… I'll be branded as a traitor. They don't tolerate alliances with outsiders, not even for the sake of strength."

Kian's face softened, his tone gentle. "And is that really fair? To sacrifice your own instincts, your own potential, just to follow rules you had no say in making?"

She swallowed, the question hitting closer than she wanted to admit. "Fair or not, it's my duty. I've spent my whole life preparing to serve my clan. I can't throw that away just because… because…"

"Because of me?" he finished, his voice barely more than a whisper.

Her heart skipped a beat, and she looked away, fighting the surge of emotions his words stirred. "Yes," she replied, her voice tight. "Because of you. And because of everything you represent—freedom, trust, the idea that I don't have to live by the rules that have always defined me."

He nodded, his expression unreadable. "Lyra, I don't want you to risk everything for me. But maybe… maybe it's worth questioning what those rules are really for. Are they truly protecting you, or are they just keeping you from discovering your own strength?"

She shook her head, frustration mingling with doubt. "It's not that simple. I can't just turn my back on my clan, on everything I was taught. And if they find out…"

Kian took a step closer, his gaze steady, unwavering. "Then don't tell them. Not yet. Let this… whatever this is… be something just between us. No one else needs to know."

Her defenses wavered, his words a quiet balm to her internal struggle. But even as the logic settled over her, she felt a pang of fear. "And what happens when this mission is over, Kian? When I return to my clan and you go back to yours? Everything we've done… it'll all be meaningless."

He looked at her, a quiet resolve in his eyes. "It doesn't have to be meaningless, Lyra. What we've shared, what we've proven together—that doesn't go away just because we're from different clans. And maybe, someday, we'll have the chance to show our people that unity can be a source of strength."

She wanted to believe him, to let herself trust in the bond they'd formed, but the fear of repercussions loomed too large. The rules of her clan were strict, unforgiving. Betrayal, even the hint of disloyalty, was met with severe consequences. And yet… being beside Kian, she felt a connection she'd never anticipated, a glimpse of a life that wasn't bound by duty alone.

After a long silence, she finally whispered, "I don't know if I'm brave enough for that."

He smiled softly, his gaze unwavering. "You're braver than you think, Lyra. And whatever you decide, I'll be here. We'll face it together, even if no one else knows."

She looked at him, her heart torn between loyalty to her clan and the undeniable bond she felt growing between them. The weight of her clan's rules and her own fears pulled her back, yet the warmth of Kian's presence urged her forward, tempting her with the idea of something beyond duty and discipline.

For now, all she could do was continue the journey, the conflict within her simmering just beneath the surface, a reminder that perhaps she was no longer the person she once thought she was. And as they walked deeper into the forest, she felt the first flickers of a new path taking shape—one that might just lead her away from everything she'd ever known.

As they moved through the forest, the air grew cooler, shadows lengthening as the light began to fade. Lyra's mind was tangled in thoughts, her heart a conflicted mess she struggled to hide.

Her steps were steady, but her pulse betrayed her, racing with a turmoil she couldn't shake. Kian, walking just beside her, seemed to sense the unease radiating from her in waves.

He glanced at her, his eyes full of quiet concern. "Lyra, you don't have to keep all of this bottled up, you know. I can see something's eating at you."

She kept her gaze forward, her voice clipped. "I'm fine, Kian. There's nothing to talk about."

He sighed, a hint of frustration slipping through his otherwise calm tone. "You don't have to do that. I'm not the enemy here. If something's weighing on you, why not let me in?"

She shot him a quick, guarded look. "Some things are just… complicated. And talking won't change that."

Kian stopped, forcing her to halt as well. He turned to face her, his eyes earnest and steady. "Then maybe it's time to look at what's really complicating things. Lyra, you don't have to be bound by rules that don't serve you."

She stiffened, feeling the familiar instinct to pull away, to retreat behind her walls. "Those rules are there for a reason, Kian. They've protected my clan for generations. Loyalty isn't something you can just throw away because it feels inconvenient."

He studied her, his gaze unwavering. "But what does loyalty really mean to you? Is it just about following rules? Or is it about something deeper?"

She hesitated, the question hitting closer than she wanted to admit. "Loyalty means putting your clan, your people, above everything else. Even yourself."

"And you think that's all it can be?" he asked softly. "What if loyalty could mean something more? Like being true to yourself, as well?"

She looked away, her tone defensive. "That's selfish. Putting myself above my duty… it's not who I am."

"Are you sure?" Kian pressed, his voice gentle but insistent. "Because the Lyra I've seen is more than just a soldier following orders. You're strong, yes, but there's so much more to you than just discipline and duty."

She let out a slow breath, feeling the weight of his words pressing on her. "What you're asking… it's impossible. My loyalty is to my clan. That's all that matters."

He tilted his head, his eyes softening. "I'm not asking you to abandon your loyalty, Lyra. I'm just asking you to consider what loyalty could mean if it included who you truly are. Not just the version your clan expects."

She clenched her fists, a flicker of frustration mixing with doubt. "It's not that simple, Kian. I can't just… change everything I believe in."

"I'm not saying you have to change everything," he replied, his tone calm. "But maybe, just maybe, you could start by questioning what's right for you. Not just what's right according to everyone else."

She looked down, her voice barely above a whisper. "And if I do that… what does that make me?"

He took a step closer, his voice soft, steady. "It makes you human, Lyra. Someone with her own thoughts, her own dreams. And someone who deserves to choose her path, not just follow one set out for her."

She felt her throat tighten, the conflicting pull between her loyalty and the quiet, unspoken longing she hadn't allowed herself to acknowledge. "I can't betray my clan, Kian. I can't."

"I'm not asking you to betray anyone," he assured her, his hand hovering near hers, close enough to feel the warmth radiating from him. "I'm just asking you to trust yourself. To trust that maybe there's a way to be loyal to your clan *and* to yourself."

Lyra swallowed, the sincerity in his gaze making her chest ache. She wanted to believe him, to let herself trust in the possibility of something beyond the narrow world she'd always known. But the thought of straying from her duty, of allowing herself to feel this pull toward him, felt like a betrayal she wasn't ready to face.

"I don't know if I can," she admitted, her voice barely more than a whisper.

Kian's smile was soft, understanding. "That's okay. I don't expect you to have all the answers now. But just... promise me you'll think about it. About what you really want."

She hesitated, her gaze meeting his, a flicker of vulnerability slipping through her usual guarded expression. "And what if what I want is... dangerous?"

He didn't look away, his voice steady. "Then maybe it's a danger worth facing."

A silence fell between them, heavy with unspoken emotions. Lyra felt a pang of fear and hope intertwined, the sense that a choice was looming, one that would shape the path ahead. She wanted to turn away, to brush off his words and retreat into the comfort of her loyalty, her discipline. But something in her held firm, resisting the urge to close herself off.

Finally, she took a deep breath, her voice barely audible. "I'll... I'll think about it."

Kian's face softened, a glimmer of warmth in his eyes. "That's all I ask."

They resumed their path in silence, but the tension between them was different now—a quiet, simmering connection that defied the boundaries she'd placed around herself. And as they walked, Lyra couldn't shake the feeling that perhaps, just perhaps, the rules she'd held so close might not be the only way forward.

Chapter 11
Visions of What Could Be

As they ventured deeper into the forest, the air grew thick and heavy, the shadows lengthening and shifting as if alive. Lyra felt a strange energy settle over her, a subtle hum that prickled against her skin. She paused, glancing around, her senses alert. This part of the forest had an otherworldly quality to it, and she felt as though she'd crossed an invisible threshold into something beyond the ordinary realm.

"Lyra?" Kian's voice cut through her thoughts, laced with concern.

She held up a hand, her gaze still sweeping over the trees. "Something's... different here."

He stepped closer, his expression cautious. "Different how?"

She took a slow, steadying breath, unsure of how to explain. "It's like... the forest is showing me something."

Just then, the air seemed to ripple before her, bending and distorting as though reality itself had thinned. In the space between two ancient trees, a vision began to take shape—a haunting image that pulled her in, her heart pounding.

It was herself, years older, standing alone in a barren landscape. Her face was set in a hard, stoic expression, her stance rigid, her eyes devoid of warmth. Around her, she saw remnants of the forest she knew, but it was a twisted version—dark and lifeless. She wore the armor of her clan, its symbols and insignia worn like a second skin, but her gaze was hollow, empty.

Lyra's throat tightened as she watched the vision unfold, unable to look away. The future version of herself moved with a mechanical precision, fulfilling her duties with unwavering focus, yet there was no spark in her eyes, no sense of purpose beyond the strict adherence to the rules that had bound her.

And then, she saw Kian.

He stood at a distance, a mere shadow in her life, as if he were a ghost or a memory she had allowed to fade. In this future, he was distant, almost invisible—a reminder of something she had never let herself fully embrace. He looked at her with a quiet sadness, his face etched with disappointment, yet he said nothing. He remained an outsider, kept at arm's length, unable to reach her.

She felt a pang of dread twist in her stomach, and her voice came out in a whisper. "Is this… my future?"

Kian, who hadn't seen the vision, noticed her distress and stepped closer, his tone gentle. "Lyra? What's wrong?"

She turned to him, her expression conflicted. "I… I saw something. A vision."

His brow furrowed. "What kind of vision?"

She took a shaky breath, struggling to articulate the weight of what she had seen. "It was me, in the future. Alone, bound to my duty. You were there, but… you weren't really there. You were just… a shadow."

Kian's face softened, his gaze filled with understanding. "And how did that make you feel?"

She hesitated, her voice barely above a whisper. "Empty. It was like… everything I'd worked for, all my dedication to my clan, had left me with nothing but isolation. I was… just a soldier, nothing more."

He reached out, his hand resting lightly on her shoulder. "Lyra, you don't have to become that version of yourself. Visions show us possibilities, not certainties."

She looked away, his words a balm she wasn't sure she deserved. "But what if it's true? What if that's what loyalty demands? What if I'm supposed to be alone?"

Kian's grip on her shoulder tightened, grounding her. "Loyalty doesn't have to mean isolation, Lyra. You can be loyal to your clan and still have a life beyond duty. You can let people in."

She shook her head, the vision's bleakness still pressing on her heart. "My clan doesn't allow that. Our rules, our traditions—they're meant to keep us strong, focused. Anything else is seen as a weakness."

Kian stepped in front of her, his eyes intense, his voice firm. "Is that what you believe? That connecting with someone, letting yourself feel, would make you weak?"

Her gaze wavered, her defenses cracking. "I don't know. I've never let myself... try."

He exhaled softly, his voice filled with quiet determination. "Then maybe it's time to find out. You have a choice, Lyra. You don't have to accept that future."

She looked up at him, a mixture of fear and hope flickering in her eyes. "But what if I fail? What if trying to have more... makes me lose everything?"

Kian's gaze softened, his tone unwavering. "Then you'll know that you tried. And maybe that's worth more than staying trapped in a life that leaves you feeling hollow."

Her throat tightened, the vision's image of her isolated, cold self seared into her memory. She could feel the pull of that future, the weight of her duty tugging her back toward the path she'd always known. But here, with Kian looking at her with such quiet conviction, she felt a glimmer of something new—a desire to break free, to find a life where she was more than just a soldier.

After a long pause, she finally whispered, "I don't want that future."

Kian's smile was warm, encouraging. "Then don't let it happen. You're stronger than you think, Lyra. And you're not alone—not unless you choose to be."

She took a steadying breath, nodding slowly. "Maybe… maybe there's a way. A way to be true to my duty without losing myself."

He nodded, his hand gently squeezing her shoulder. "Exactly. And if you need help figuring that out… I'm here."

As they resumed their journey, the vision lingered in Lyra's mind, a reminder of the path she didn't want to take. For the first time, she felt a quiet determination to forge her own way forward, even if it meant challenging everything she had been taught. And as Kian walked beside her, she couldn't shake the feeling that maybe, just maybe, he was the key to a future she hadn't dared to dream of before.

The forest path narrowed as they walked, and Lyra found herself casting sidelong glances at Kian, her mind still echoing with the vision she'd seen. The image of herself, so cold and alone, felt like a warning—a glimpse of a future shaped entirely by duty, devoid of anything else. It lingered, unsettling her deeply. And though she was hesitant, a question had taken root in her thoughts, one that refused to be ignored.

"Kian," she began softly, surprising even herself with the vulnerability in her voice.

He looked at her, his expression open, a gentle curiosity in his eyes. "Yes?"

She hesitated, struggling to find the words. "Why is freedom so important to you? I mean... why would you choose it over duty?"

He tilted his head thoughtfully, a faint smile crossing his face. "I think that's the first time you've asked me about something personal."

She shot him a quick, defensive look. "Don't read too much into it. I'm just... curious."

Kian's smile softened, and he nodded. "Fair enough. Well, for me, freedom isn't just about doing what I want. It's about living a life that feels true. A life where I'm not just following orders or bound by expectations that don't make sense to me."

Lyra frowned, her voice laced with uncertainty. "But doesn't that get... chaotic? Without structure, without rules, how do you know you're doing the right thing?"

He looked away, his gaze drifting to the path ahead, his voice reflective. "It's not always easy. Freedom comes with its own challenges, and sometimes I question myself, sure. But I'd rather face those doubts and make my own choices than live by rules that someone else set for me. Rules that don't feel... right."

She absorbed his words, her mind racing. "So you're saying that duty isn't... enough?"

He looked back at her, his expression gentle but resolute. "Duty has its place. But if it starts to consume you, if it takes away your ability to choose your own path, then what's the point? A life spent only following orders… it's like you're not living for yourself. You're just… existing."

She let his words settle, feeling the familiar weight of her clan's teachings press down on her. "In my clan, duty is everything. It's what defines us, gives us purpose. Without it, we'd be… lost."

Kian nodded, his gaze sympathetic. "I get that. But isn't it possible to have duty *and* choice? To find a balance where you can honor your clan without losing yourself?"

Her brow furrowed as she looked down, her fingers tracing patterns in the dirt. "I've never thought of it that way. I always assumed loyalty meant… giving everything. Not questioning, not second-guessing."

"Loyalty doesn't have to mean blind obedience," he said, his voice calm but insistent. "It can mean standing by those you care about, supporting them because you choose to, not just because you're told to. It's a choice, Lyra. And that makes it even stronger."

She looked up at him, something shifting within her, the faintest crack in the walls she'd kept so carefully guarded. "And what if… if choosing to honor myself means going against what my clan expects?"

Kian's eyes softened, his tone encouraging. "Then that's where you decide what loyalty truly means to you. Maybe it means finding your own way to serve them, even if it looks different from what they're used to. It doesn't have to be all or nothing."

She took a deep breath, the possibility both freeing and terrifying. "You make it sound easy."

"It's not," he replied with a faint smile. "Trust me, I know that better than anyone. Freedom has its own risks, and I've made plenty of mistakes. But I'd rather make those mistakes and learn from them than live a life that doesn't feel like my own."

Lyra's gaze drifted away, the weight of his words settling in her chest, stirring questions she'd never allowed herself to consider. "I don't know if I'm brave enough for that. My whole life has been about following the rules, doing what's expected."

Kian stepped closer, his eyes searching hers, warm with quiet support. "But you're already braver than you think, Lyra. You're questioning, reflecting. And that takes more courage than simply following orders."

She looked at him, her heart aching with the realization that he might be right. "You really believe that?"

He nodded, a smile flickering across his face. "Absolutely. You have strength, Lyra. And maybe now, you're finding the courage to choose what that strength looks like, instead of letting someone else define it for you."

For a long moment, they stood there in silence, the forest surrounding them, the weight of her clan's expectations and Kian's quiet confidence mingling in her mind. The path ahead was uncertain, and the future loomed, filled with choices she hadn't been prepared to make.

But for the first time, she felt a glimmer of hope that perhaps, she didn't have to walk it alone. And as she looked at Kian, she knew that he was helping her see the possibilities beyond the life she'd always known—a life where freedom and duty might not be mutually exclusive after all.

The shadows around them seemed to thicken, gathering like storm clouds as Lyra and Kian continued down the narrow forest path. The air grew colder, laced with an eerie stillness that set Lyra's nerves on edge. She felt the familiar weight of her blade at her side, her grip tightening in anticipation as her eyes scanned the deepening darkness.

It was then that the first creature emerged, its form twisting and writhing, a mass of shadows that seemed to defy any single shape. Its eyes glowed with a fierce, predatory hunger, and Lyra could feel a cold dread settle over her—a reminder of the darkness she carried within herself, the struggle between duty and desire that had haunted her since her vision.

"Kian," she said, her voice tense, her gaze never leaving the creature.

He moved beside her, his flame springing to life, casting a warm glow that pushed back the encroaching shadows. "I see it. And I have a feeling it's not alone."

As if in response, more shadow creatures appeared from the trees, their movements silent but swift, their eyes fixed on the two of them. Lyra felt her heartbeat quicken, and she drew her blade, the familiar weight grounding her as she steadied her stance.

"These things…" she murmured, almost to herself. "They're relentless."

Kian nodded, his tone grim. "And they're not just after us physically. It's almost as if they're feeding off something deeper."

Lyra cast him a quick, searching look. "What do you mean?"

He met her gaze, his voice low. "These shadows—don't they feel like they're a part of what we're fighting within ourselves? Our fears, our doubts?"

For a moment, Lyra hesitated, the truth of his words settling over her. These creatures, born from darkness, felt like an extension of the turmoil she carried inside—the fear of abandoning her duty, the pull toward something beyond what she'd always known. But she didn't have time to dwell on it, as the creatures advanced, their twisted forms closing in on them.

With a swift motion, she lunged at the nearest creature, her blade slicing through the shadows, only for it to reform, tendrils lashing out toward her. She deflected the attack, her movements quick, precise, each strike fueled by the discipline she'd relied on her entire life. But these creatures seemed to adapt, each one more relentless than the last.

Beside her, Kian fought with a fierce intensity, his flames searing through the creatures, forcing them back. The fire and shadows collided, intertwining in a chaotic dance that seemed to shift and blend their powers. She felt her own shadows instinctively reacting to his flames, creating a synergy that was both powerful and strange, their abilities enhancing each other in ways she hadn't anticipated.

"Lyra!" Kian called out, his voice cutting through the fray. "On your left!"

She turned just in time to see a creature lunging at her, its claws extended. Without hesitation, she sidestepped, slashing her blade through its form, while Kian's flames surged forward, consuming the creature in a burst of fire. Their movements flowed together seamlessly, each relying on the other's strength, their instincts aligned in a way that felt almost... natural.

As they fought, Lyra found herself drawn into a rhythm with him, their powers blending in perfect harmony. She felt her shadows responding to his flame, amplifying its heat, creating a barrier that the creatures struggled to penetrate. And for the first time, she felt a strange peace in the chaos of battle—a sense that, with Kian beside her, she wasn't fighting alone.

But as another wave of creatures emerged, Lyra's thoughts flickered back to her clan, to the duty that had always defined her. This connection, this reliance on someone else—it was against everything she'd been taught. Yet here she was, trusting him implicitly, her every movement attuned to his, the walls she'd so carefully built slipping further with each strike they shared.

"Lyra," Kian said, his voice breaking through her thoughts as they pushed back the last of the creatures. "You're not fighting this battle alone, you know."

She caught her breath, her gaze still wary. "I'm not used to fighting alongside anyone. It's… different."

"Different isn't bad," he replied, his gaze warm, steady. "Sometimes, it's what makes us stronger."

She looked away, feeling the familiar tension rise within her, the reminder of her duty, her loyalty to her clan. "Strength isn't about relying on others. It's about discipline, control. That's what I've always known."

Kian's expression softened, a quiet understanding in his eyes. "But what if strength can also mean connection? Trusting someone else doesn't make you weaker, Lyra. It doesn't take away from who you are—it just… adds to it."

She didn't respond, her gaze fixed on the dissipating shadows that lingered where the creatures had been. Part of her wanted to reject his words, to cling to the certainty of her clan's teachings. But another part—a part that felt more like herself than she'd ever allowed—wanted to believe him.

They stood in silence, the weight of their battle lingering in the air, as well as the questions it had stirred. And though Lyra didn't speak, the warmth of Kian's presence beside her, steady and unyielding, was a reminder that maybe, just maybe, there was strength in embracing the light and shadows within herself, especially with him by her side.

The echoes of the battle faded, and the forest settled back into its usual stillness. Shadows lingered, cast by the sinking sun, but the creatures were gone, leaving only silence and the soft rustling of leaves in their wake. Lyra and Kian stood side by side, catching their breath, their gazes drifting to the horizon, where night slowly claimed the sky.

Kian broke the silence first, his tone calm but resolute. "You know, Lyra, there's more to life than what you've been taught. You don't have to live by their rules forever."

She stiffened, turning to him, her eyes narrowing slightly. "My clan's rules are what keep us strong. Without them, we'd be lost."

"Or maybe," he said, his gaze unwavering, "you'd be free."

She frowned, the conflict within her flaring once more. "Freedom isn't always what it seems, Kian. It comes with risks, with uncertainty. My clan offers stability, purpose. There's value in that."

He took a step closer, his voice soft but insistent. "But what about you, Lyra? Where are *you* in all of that? Are you just an extension of their rules, or are you someone beyond them?"

She looked away, her gaze fixed on the ground as her fingers brushed over the hilt of her blade, the symbol of everything she'd been taught to believe in. "I don't know," she murmured. "I've always thought of myself as a part of something greater. As if my identity didn't matter beyond serving my clan."

Kian's hand found her shoulder, grounding her with a gentle squeeze. "But it does matter. You matter. Don't you deserve to find out who you are, beyond their expectations?"

Her jaw tightened, an instinctive resistance rising within her, yet his words lingered, pressing against her carefully constructed resolve. "You make it sound so simple. Just walk away from everything I've known? My loyalty isn't something I can just… let go of."

He nodded, his voice understanding but firm. "I'm not asking you to let go of loyalty. I'm asking you to redefine it. Maybe loyalty doesn't mean sacrificing yourself entirely. Maybe it can mean honoring your duty while also honoring who you truly are."

Lyra swallowed, feeling the weight of his words settle over her, cracking the walls she'd built piece by piece. "That sounds like a risk my clan wouldn't understand. They'd see it as weakness."

"Or maybe," he replied, his eyes meeting hers with quiet conviction, "they'd see it as strength. The strength to be more than just one thing. To be someone who's willing to look beyond tradition and see what else life has to offer."

She took a step back, her gaze troubled. "And what if I find that what I want… isn't what they want?"

Kian's expression softened, his voice filled with understanding. "Then maybe that's okay. Maybe it's about finding a balance between their expectations and your own path."

She looked away, wrestling with the emotions swirling within her. The vision of a lonely, duty-bound future flashed in her mind—a future where she was nothing more than a vessel for her clan's rules, devoid of any personal dreams or desires. That image unsettled her deeply, yet stepping beyond that life felt like stepping off a ledge into the unknown.

Kian's words cut through her thoughts, steady and grounding. "Lyra, you've followed every rule, upheld every expectation. You've proven your loyalty a hundred times over. Maybe now it's time to think about what *you* want."

Her voice was quiet, almost a whisper. "I don't even know what that is."

He smiled gently, his tone filled with encouragement. "Then maybe that's where you start. Just… be open to the possibility. You don't have to decide everything now. Just let yourself think about what a life beyond the rules might look like."

She met his gaze, her resolve softening even as the uncertainty remained. "You make it sound so… possible."

"Because it is," he replied simply. "And no matter what you choose, I'll be here. You don't have to face this alone."

The warmth in his eyes, the quiet promise in his words—it made her feel something she hadn't allowed herself to feel in a long time: hope. Hope that maybe, just maybe, she could carve out a path that was truly her own, even if it meant challenging the rules she'd always known.

They continued forward, and though Lyra didn't voice her doubts, the weight of his words lingered. The forest stretched out before them, dark and unknown, mirroring the uncertainty of the choices that lay ahead. Yet for the first time, she felt a quiet, tentative openness to the idea that perhaps there was more to life than duty—and that Kian might be the one to help her discover it.

Chapter 12
A Choice Deferred

As Lyra walked through the dense forest, an unfamiliar tension settled over her. Shadows danced in the fading light, and the trees seemed to loom closer, their branches weaving an intricate canopy above. She felt the forest pressing in on her, as if guiding her toward something she'd been avoiding, something hidden deep within her heart.

Without warning, the air thickened, a strange energy crackling around her. Lyra stopped, sensing she was once again on the edge of something powerful, something that had already revealed so many buried truths. She took a deep, steadying breath, but before she could center herself, the world around her shifted.

In front of her, a vision began to take shape, shimmering as if reflected in water. It was her, yet it wasn't—the figure that stood before her was softer somehow, her face unguarded, her posture relaxed, and her eyes bright with a spark Lyra couldn't quite recognize. This version of herself wore no armor, no insignia of her clan, and her stance was free of the rigidity Lyra had worn like a second skin her entire life.

Lyra's throat tightened, her voice coming out barely above a whisper. "Who... who are you?"

The reflection met her gaze, a faint, knowing smile tugging at her lips. "I'm you, Lyra. The part of you you've tried so hard to silence."

Lyra's heart pounded, her defenses instinctively rising. "I don't understand. I don't... I don't want anything else. My duty is my life."

The reflection's smile softened, her eyes filled with a quiet, unyielding truth. "Is it really? Or have you just convinced yourself of that because it's easier than facing what you truly want?"

Lyra took a step back, her voice sharpening. "What I want doesn't matter. I'm loyal to my clan, to my people. That's all I've ever known."

The reflection tilted her head, an understanding gleam in her eyes. "Loyalty doesn't have to mean losing yourself. Somewhere along the way, you decided that your clan's rules were all you could ever be, all you could ever need. But that's not the truth, is it?"

A flicker of frustration surged within her, mingling with an undeniable pang of fear. "What are you saying? That I should abandon everything? Turn my back on the people who raised me?"

"Not abandon," the reflection said gently. "But consider what it would be like to have more. To let yourself be someone who isn't only defined by duty."

Lyra clenched her fists, a sense of vulnerability she wasn't used to seizing her chest. "This... this is ridiculous. I can't just change who I am."

The reflection stepped closer, her voice soft but insistent. "You're not changing who you are. You're discovering who you've always been, under all those expectations, all those rules. Can't you feel it? That part of you that yearns to be free?"

Lyra's gaze dropped, a quiet war raging inside her. She could feel the pull of this vision, the truth in her words, but the thought of embracing it terrified her. She thought of her clan, of the life she'd lived up until now, and of everything she had sacrificed to be the perfect warrior.

"What if... what if I'm nothing without the rules? What if I'm just... lost?" she whispered, barely able to voice the fear that had haunted her for so long.

The reflection's expression softened, a hint of sadness in her eyes. "You won't be lost, Lyra. You'll be whole. You'll be more than just a soldier. You'll be someone who chose her own path, who dared to find her own meaning."

Lyra looked up, meeting her reflection's gaze, her heart heavy with longing and hesitation. She felt the weight of her clan's expectations pressing down on her, yet within her chest, a spark of something unfamiliar stirred—a quiet, undeniable yearning for freedom.

"But what if this isn't real?" she asked, her voice wavering. "What if I'm just... imagining a life that doesn't exist?"

The reflection reached out, a gentle, reassuring presence. "It's real if you let it be. You have a choice, Lyra. You don't have to walk the path laid out for you. You can make your own, even if it looks different from what you thought it should be."

Lyra closed her eyes, her mind swirling with the vision's words. She could feel the walls around her heart cracking, the life she'd known slipping away as a new possibility opened up before her—a life of choice, of purpose she defined herself, of freedom. And yet, the fear of letting go, of stepping into the unknown, held her back.

When she opened her eyes, the vision had faded, leaving only the quiet of the forest and the whisper of her own heart.

She took a deep breath, feeling both lighter and more burdened than ever. She wasn't ready to let go of everything she knew, but a part of her knew, deep down, that the yearning she felt could no longer be ignored. She didn't have to have all the answers now, but perhaps, just perhaps, she could take the first step toward finding them.

And as she continued down the path, Lyra felt a small, quiet resolve building within her—a determination to discover who she truly was, beyond the rules that had defined her life.

The forest grew denser around them, branches arching overhead like silent witnesses to the struggle building within Lyra. She felt the weight of her recent vision pressing down on her, a reminder of the possibility she hadn't wanted to face. Her thoughts were still tangled when Kian stepped beside her, his presence grounding yet disconcerting, as if he could sense the turmoil brewing within her.

He studied her carefully, his gaze unwavering. "Lyra, are you really content living like this? Always bound by rules that don't let you be yourself?"

Her head snapped up, anger flashing in her eyes. "What do you know about my life, Kian? About what I've sacrificed for my clan?"

He didn't flinch, his voice calm but firm. "I know you're stronger than anyone I've ever met. But I also know that strength shouldn't mean losing yourself. Is this really what you want? To spend your life carrying out someone else's vision of who you're supposed to be?"

Her hands clenched into fists, her voice rising. "My clan's vision is my vision. Loyalty, discipline—those things matter to me. They've given my life meaning."

He shook his head, his gaze challenging. "But at what cost, Lyra? What have you given up to fit into a role they decided for you?"

She felt the familiar sting of defensiveness, her words snapping out before she could stop herself. "I haven't given up anything. I've chosen this life because it's where I belong. My duty is everything."

"Is it, though?" he pressed, stepping closer, his gaze searching hers. "Or is it just the easiest way to ignore what you really want?"

She scoffed, anger flaring to cover the uncertainty gnawing at her. "And what would you know about duty? You don't understand—my clan has rules for a reason. They keep us focused, strong. Without them, we'd be... lost."

Kian's face softened, but his tone remained firm. "Rules don't make you strong, Lyra. You do. And if you can't be yourself within your clan, then maybe they're the ones who are lost, not you."

Her jaw tightened, her voice cold. "How dare you? You have no idea what my clan means to me, what I've been through to earn their trust."

He nodded, his gaze filled with quiet empathy. "I don't doubt your loyalty, Lyra. But I see you now—this version of you who's questioning, who's thinking for herself. And I have to wonder, is that such a bad thing?"

She looked away, frustration mingling with a raw, unspoken fear. "It's not that simple. You think I can just... walk away from everything I've known? Turn my back on the people who raised me?"

Kian's voice softened, but the conviction in his words was unyielding. "I'm not asking you to turn your back on them. But I am asking if you've ever thought about what it would mean to be true to yourself, not just to them."

Her voice shook as she met his gaze, her anger barely concealing the conflict beneath. "What I want doesn't matter, Kian. It never has. My purpose is to serve, to be part of something greater than myself."

"But what if being part of something greater doesn't mean losing yourself in it?" he asked, his tone almost a whisper. "What if it means bringing your whole self, all of you, even the parts they don't see?"

She let out a bitter laugh, her voice harsh. "And then what? They'd call me a traitor, say I'd failed them. I'd be cast out, alone."

Kian stepped closer, his gaze steady, unwavering. "You wouldn't be alone, Lyra. Not if you chose to find your own path. You'd have me. And maybe, just maybe, you'd have yourself, too."

Her breath caught, the words stirring something deep within her, a mixture of longing and fear that she couldn't contain. "This isn't about you, Kian. This is my life, my clan. You can't just… walk in and change everything."

He sighed, his voice filled with quiet understanding. "I'm not trying to change you. I just want you to see that there's more to you than the role you've been forced to play. That maybe you're worth more than the sacrifices you've been making."

She swallowed hard, her gaze faltering as she struggled to maintain her anger. "You think it's that easy? To just… let go of everything?"

"No," he replied gently, "I don't think it's easy at all. But I think it might be worth it. And I think, deep down, you're starting to see that, too."

Lyra looked away, her defenses crumbling under the weight of his words. She wanted to deny it, to push him away, but the truth of his questions lingered, impossible to ignore. For so long, she had defined herself by the rules of her clan, by her duty and loyalty. Yet here she was, faced with the possibility that those rules might be keeping her from the life she truly wanted—a life she hadn't even allowed herself to imagine.

Finally, her voice came out in a whisper, barely audible. "I don't know if I'm ready for that."

Kian nodded, his gaze filled with quiet compassion. "Then take your time. But just remember, Lyra, you're not bound by their rules. You're free to find your own way, whenever you're ready."

She didn't respond, her heart pounding as his words settled over her. The anger and defensiveness faded, replaced by a quiet, unsettling realization. The life she'd known was no longer the only path she saw before her. And though she wasn't ready to embrace it, a small part of her couldn't ignore the spark of hope Kian's words had ignited—a spark that, perhaps, one day, might grow into something more.

The forest was silent, an eerie calm settling over the twisted trees and underbrush. Lyra could feel the weight of her conversation with Kian still hanging in the air, her mind a tangle of conflicting emotions. But the forest gave her no time to dwell on them. A faint rustling echoed from the shadows, a warning that something dark and menacing lurked just beyond sight.

"Kian," she murmured, her voice tight with tension.

He was already at her side, his flames flickering to life in his hands, casting a warm glow against the approaching darkness. "I feel it too. They're coming."

Before either of them could prepare further, the shadows shifted, coalescing into dark, sinuous forms that slithered and lunged forward. These creatures were different—larger, faster, more menacing than before. Lyra drew her blade, her body instinctively falling into a fighting stance, but a sliver of doubt lodged itself in her mind, its grip tightening.

The first creature struck, its dark, shadowy claws swiping toward her with a deadly precision. Lyra barely deflected the blow, her own shadow powers meeting the creature's, forcing it back. But it wasn't enough. These shadows were relentless, moving in perfect sync, feeding off the darkness that pooled in her own heart—her doubts, her fears, her questions.

She struck again, her blade slicing through one of the creatures, but another surged forward, and for a heart-stopping moment, she realized she was surrounded.

"Kian!" she called out, her voice edged with desperation.

Without hesitation, he moved to her side, his flames bursting forward in a fierce, protective barrier that drove the shadows back. "I'm here, Lyra. We've got this."

They fought together, their powers weaving in and out of each other like threads in a tapestry. Her shadows and his flames clashed against the creatures, creating bursts of light and dark that illuminated the forest in flashes. But the creatures didn't relent; they seemed to grow stronger, each strike feeding off her inner conflict, her wavering resolve.

One of the creatures lunged at her from the left, slipping through a gap in her defenses. Lyra swung her blade, but her timing was off—her movements slower, weighed down by the doubts gnawing at her focus.

Kian was there in an instant, his flames igniting in a brilliant flash that sent the creature reeling. He turned to her, his voice filled with concern. "Lyra, are you okay?"

She nodded, her breath coming in ragged gasps. "Yes, I... I'm fine." But the words felt hollow. She knew, in that moment, that without him, she wouldn't have survived the attack. And the realization hit her like a blow to the chest.

They continued to fight, but the thought lingered, her mind racing as she parried another attack. *Without him, I wouldn't be here right now. Without Kian, I wouldn't have the strength to face this.*

It was an uncomfortable truth, one that tore at the very foundation of her beliefs. She had always prided herself on her independence, her self-reliance. But now, here she was, fighting alongside someone whose strength complemented her own, whose presence steadied her in ways she hadn't allowed herself to acknowledge.

As they fended off the last of the creatures, Lyra felt a strange calm settle over her. Her heart still pounded, but the realization brought with it an undeniable clarity.

Once the shadows had dissipated, Kian turned to her, his face etched with concern. "You looked… distracted back there. What's going on?"

She hesitated, her voice quiet, almost fragile. "I realized something. Without you, I don't think I would have made it through that fight."

Kian gave her a soft, reassuring smile. "You're stronger than you give yourself credit for, Lyra. But sometimes, strength isn't about standing alone. It's about knowing when to lean on someone else."

Her gaze dropped, the weight of his words settling over her. "That goes against everything I was taught. My clan… they taught me to rely on myself, to never depend on anyone else."

"But maybe," he said gently, his tone filled with quiet conviction, "they forgot to teach you that real strength can come from connection, too."

She looked up, meeting his eyes, a quiet vulnerability in her own. "I don't know if I'm ready to believe that."

He reached out, his hand resting lightly on her shoulder. "You don't have to believe it all at once. Just… let yourself see what it feels like. Because right now, we're stronger together than we could ever be alone."

Lyra felt her resolve waver, the walls she'd built around her heart crumbling with each passing moment. The battle with the shadow creatures had forced her to confront the truth she'd been denying: that Kian was more than just an ally—he was her strength, a part of herself she hadn't known was missing.

Taking a shaky breath, she nodded, her voice barely above a whisper. "Thank you, Kian. For being here."

He smiled, a warmth in his eyes that eased the last of her resistance. "Always, Lyra. I'll be here as long as you'll let me."

They stood in silence, the remnants of the battle fading around them. And though the doubts still lingered, Lyra felt a glimmer of hope—a hope that, maybe, she could forge a path that was hers alone, with someone by her side to face the shadows, both outside and within.

The forest was quiet again, the shadows retreating into the depths, leaving only the faint rustle of leaves in the evening breeze. Lyra's body ached from the battle, each step feeling heavier than the last as she and Kian made their way to a small clearing. She sank to the ground, exhaustion settling over her like a weight she couldn't shake. Her breaths came in shallow, ragged bursts, but it wasn't just the fight that had worn her down; it was everything that came with it—the choices she knew were waiting, the path that lay before her, branching in two directions.

Kian sat beside her, his presence steady and grounding. He didn't speak at first, letting the silence stretch between them, a quiet understanding that he knew she needed space to process. But even without words, she could feel the warmth of his support, a reminder of the connection that had grown between them—a bond that had surprised her, challenged her, and left her questioning everything she'd ever believed.

Finally, he broke the silence, his voice gentle. "You did well back there. Those creatures… they didn't stand a chance against you."

Lyra managed a faint smile, though it didn't quite reach her eyes. "Only because you were there. I… I needed you."

He glanced at her, his gaze soft but unwavering. "And I needed you, Lyra. That's what makes us stronger. Together."

She looked away, her fingers tracing patterns in the dirt as she tried to quell the turmoil in her heart. "I was never taught that. Needing someone else… it was always seen as a weakness."

"Then maybe it's time to question what you were taught," he replied, his tone laced with quiet conviction. "Because I don't see weakness in you. I see strength, courage. I see someone who's finding her own way, even if it's hard."

She let out a long breath, the weight of his words sinking in. Her clan's rules, her duty—those had been her guiding principles, the anchor that had defined her life. She had been raised to serve, to honor the rules above all else, to stand alone as a pillar of strength for her people. But now, that foundation felt unsteady, the clarity of purpose she'd once had clouded by the bond she shared with Kian.

It wasn't that her loyalty to her clan had disappeared. It was still there, fierce and unwavering. But the path she'd been walking—the one dictated by her clan's traditions—no longer felt complete. She could feel a pull toward something more, something she hadn't allowed herself to imagine until now.

Her voice was barely a whisper as she spoke, the vulnerability raw and unfamiliar. "I don't know if I can choose, Kian. My clan… they're my family, my purpose. I owe them everything."

Kian nodded, his expression understanding. "And no one's asking you to turn your back on them. But maybe, just maybe, there's a way to honor your clan while also honoring what you're discovering within yourself."

She looked at him, her heart aching with the weight of it all. "What if there isn't? What if I have to choose?"

He reached out, his hand gently covering hers. "Then choose the path that feels true to you, Lyra. Not the one you were told to walk, but the one that lets you be who you really are."

She stared down at their hands, his warmth grounding her, and for a moment, she let herself consider it—a life beyond the strict confines of her clan's rules, a life where she could define her own strength, her own loyalty. The thought terrified her, yet it filled her with a quiet, fragile hope.

A soft breeze swept through the clearing, and as she closed her eyes, she felt the tug of both paths, her clan's traditions on one side and this newfound connection on the other. Each one called to her, demanding a part of her heart, her soul. She knew that whatever choice she made, it would define her, not just as a warrior, but as a person.

Opening her eyes, she met Kian's gaze, her voice steady but laced with uncertainty. "I don't have the answers yet. I'm not ready to decide."

He smiled, a quiet acceptance in his eyes. "Then don't. Take the time you need. Whatever you choose, Lyra, know that I'm here, whether you walk beside me or find your own path."

A silence fell between them, filled with unspoken understanding. And as Lyra sat beside him, the forest settling into the deepening twilight, she knew that the choice would not come easily. But for the first time, she felt ready to face it—not as a soldier bound by duty, but as herself, a woman learning to listen to her own heart, and the path it longed to follow.

Chapter 13
At the Crossroads

The forest was quiet, a gentle breeze rustling through the leaves, carrying with it the faint scent of pine and earth. Lyra walked beside Kian, her heart pounding louder than she cared to admit. Every time she stole a glance at him, a surge of unfamiliar warmth spread through her chest, an ache she couldn't quite ignore. She'd tried to dismiss it, to push it down and bury it beneath her duty, her loyalty to her clan, but with each passing day, that pull between them had only grown stronger.

Kian noticed her silence and shot her a sideways glance, a hint of amusement dancing in his eyes. "You're awfully quiet, Lyra. Something on your mind?"

She hesitated, her fingers brushing against the hilt of her blade, a familiar gesture that usually steadied her. But today, it didn't. "No, it's… it's nothing."

He chuckled, a soft sound that sent a shiver down her spine. "Lyra, you're a lot of things, but subtle isn't one of them. There's something you're not saying."

She turned away, hoping the cool air might calm the warmth rising in her cheeks. "I don't know what you're talking about."

"Sure you don't," he replied, his tone playful but with a note of sincerity. "Look, I get it. Letting yourself feel… it's new for you. It's scary."

She shot him a quick, guarded look, her voice defensive. "I never said I was scared."

"No, but you don't have to," he replied gently, his gaze steady on her. "I can see it. You're worried. Maybe about what this means, or maybe about what it could lead to."

Lyra's throat tightened, his words striking closer to the truth than she wanted to admit. She felt a flicker of frustration, a need to put distance between them, to protect herself. "You're assuming a lot, Kian. This… whatever this is… it doesn't change anything."

His expression softened, the teasing gone, replaced by quiet understanding. "Doesn't it? You're allowed to care, Lyra. It doesn't make you weak. And it doesn't mean you're any less loyal to your clan."

She looked down, her voice barely a whisper. "You don't understand. If I let myself… feel this, if I let you in… it changes everything."

Kian nodded, his tone gentle. "I know. But sometimes, change isn't as dangerous as we think. Sometimes, it's exactly what we need."

Lyra let out a shaky breath, the weight of her clan's expectations pressing down on her. "You say that because you don't know the consequences. In my world, affection is a risk, a distraction. It's seen as weakness."

"And maybe that's where they're wrong," he replied, his voice unwavering. "Caring for someone doesn't make you weak, Lyra. It makes you stronger. It gives you something to fight for, something worth protecting."

She looked up at him, her defenses faltering as she met his gaze. "I don't know how to balance that. How to care for someone without losing sight of my purpose."

Kian smiled, his expression warm and reassuring. "Maybe you don't have to balance it perfectly. Maybe it's enough to let yourself feel, to see where it leads. No one's asking you to change who you are, Lyra. Just… to let yourself be human."

Her heart pounded, his words settling over her like a gentle wave, eroding the edges of her resistance. "What if I don't want to be human? What if that makes me vulnerable, distracted?"

He shook his head, his gaze filled with quiet confidence. "Maybe a little vulnerability is what makes us whole. What keeps us grounded."

She looked away, her voice barely more than a whisper. "This is dangerous, Kian. For both of us."

He took a step closer, his hand hovering near hers, close enough to feel his warmth. "I know. And I'm willing to face that danger if you are."

Lyra's chest tightened, the fear and longing swirling within her, a potent mix she wasn't sure she could handle. She wanted to push him away, to deny the feelings that were stirring, but the quiet acceptance in his gaze, the understanding he offered without judgment, made her want to stay. Made her want to let herself believe that maybe, just maybe, caring for him didn't make her weaker—it made her more.

She swallowed, her voice steady but laced with a vulnerability she hadn't allowed herself to feel. "I don't know where this leads, Kian. I don't know if I can risk everything for… something I don't understand."

Kian's smile was soft, his voice a whisper. "Then let's not rush it. Let's just… see what happens. Together."

For a long moment, they stood in silence, the forest a quiet witness to their unspoken bond. And though she still felt the weight of her clan's expectations pressing down on her, Lyra couldn't ignore the glimmer of hope that Kian's words had sparked. It was a hope that maybe, she could be both strong and vulnerable, loyal and free.

And as they continued down the path, she let herself hold onto that possibility, even if just for a moment.

As they walked through the forest, the path ahead stretched into shadowed unknowns, mirroring the uncertainty swirling within Lyra. The silence between her and Kian was thick, yet comfortable, as if they both understood the weight of what wasn't being said. With each step, her mind wrestled with a question she couldn't ignore any longer—a question that felt heavier than any blade she'd ever carried.

"Lyra," Kian's voice broke through her thoughts, his tone gentle. "You're lost in your head again. I can tell."

She glanced at him, forcing a small, distracted smile. "I'm just... thinking."

"About?" he prompted, his gaze steady, patient.

Lyra hesitated, her words slow and careful. "About everything. My clan. This journey. You."

He nodded, sensing her inner turmoil. "You're questioning things that you've never questioned before. And that's not easy."

She sighed, her voice barely above a whisper. "I don't know if I'm strong enough to do it. My whole life, I've been told who I am, what my purpose is. I was raised to be loyal, to serve. And now... I'm starting to wonder if there's more to me than just that."

Kian's expression softened, a quiet understanding in his gaze. "And what if there is? What if you could still be loyal to your clan but also honor who you truly are?"

Her fists clenched at her sides, the frustration building. "But that's just it, Kian. My clan sees loyalty as absolute. It doesn't leave room for questions, for... anything else. I've been trained to shut down anything that doesn't align with duty."

"And now that you're letting yourself feel something different," he said slowly, "it scares you."

She looked away, her voice raw with vulnerability. "Yes. Because I don't know where it leads. I don't know who I am without those rules."

Kian moved closer, his voice gentle but firm. "You don't have to abandon loyalty, Lyra. But maybe it's time to redefine what loyalty means for you. It doesn't have to be one or the other—you can still be committed to your clan, but make room for yourself, too."

Her gaze shifted to the forest floor, her thoughts a tangled mess. "But what if my clan doesn't accept that? What if they see it as betrayal?"

"Then that's a choice they make," he replied, his voice steady. "But you... you have the right to choose who you want to be. Even if it's different from what they expect."

She swallowed, her heart heavy with the weight of his words. "You make it sound so simple. But the truth is, I don't even know where to start."

Kian smiled, a soft, encouraging warmth in his gaze. "Start by allowing yourself to keep walking this path. With me. Let's take it one step at a time. You don't have to make a decision right now."

Her chest tightened, a blend of fear and hope stirring within her. "But what if following this path with you takes me further away from my clan? From everything I've ever known?"

He looked at her, his gaze unwavering. "Then maybe you'll find something new along the way. Something that feels right for *you*, not just for them."

She took a deep breath, her resolve wavering. "You really believe that's possible?"

"Yes," he said simply. "Because you're already doing it, Lyra. Every day you're choosing to question, to feel, to think beyond the life they set for you. That's the first step."

For a moment, she let herself consider his words, the possibility of a life where she could be both loyal to her clan and true to herself. It felt distant, almost unattainable, yet the thought of turning back now, of letting go of this newfound sense of self, filled her with a quiet dread.

Kian's voice was soft but insistent. "You don't have to have all the answers yet. Just let yourself keep going. See where it leads."

She looked up at him, the depth of her internal struggle clear in her eyes. "And if I fail? If I can't find a way to be both?"

"Then we'll face that when the time comes," he replied gently. "But for now, let yourself be here. Let yourself try."

Lyra nodded slowly, her defenses slipping as she allowed herself to breathe, to be present. She knew the road ahead was uncertain, the questions she faced complex and painful. But for the first time, she felt a spark of possibility—a faint glimmer of a life where she didn't have to sacrifice one part of herself to honor another.

They continued down the path, and though her heart still held the weight of doubt, Lyra knew that as long as she kept moving, she was finding her own way—one step at a time, with Kian beside her.

The forest had grown darker, the sunlight filtering weakly through the thick canopy above as Lyra and Kian continued down the winding path. The quiet between them was comfortable, punctuated by the occasional snap of twigs underfoot or the distant call of birds. But beneath the surface, Lyra's thoughts churned, the decision she knew she would soon have to make looming over her like a shadow.

Just as she was beginning to calm, she heard it—a faint rustle, the unmistakable sound of footsteps moving in practiced unison. Her heart leapt into her throat, her body going rigid as she recognized the cadence of her clan's patrol, their movements as disciplined and precise as her own. She instinctively reached out, gripping Kian's arm, pulling him off the path and into the thick cover of the trees.

"Lyra?" he whispered, his voice barely audible as they crouched behind a wide, moss-covered trunk.

"Shh," she breathed, pressing a finger to her lips. "It's my clan."

His eyes widened in understanding, and he nodded, his face shadowed with concern. They both fell silent, listening as the patrol drew nearer. Lyra's pulse thundered in her ears, a cold sweat prickling her skin. The familiar voices drifted closer, snippets of conversation carried on the breeze. Her breath caught as she recognized one of them—Kara, a fierce warrior she'd trained beside for years, someone she'd once called a friend.

"What's the report?" Kara's voice was firm, carrying a hint of impatience.

"Nothing unusual," another voice replied. "But the council's concerned. They've heard rumors of… outsiders."

Lyra's heart twisted painfully. She knew the weight her clan placed on loyalty, the unforgiving stance they took on outsiders and those who associated with them. To be seen with Kian here, in this moment, would mean not only punishment for herself but potentially exile. The thought chilled her, and she glanced at Kian, who was watching her with a mixture of concern and understanding.

"They're close," he whispered, his gaze steady. "But we'll be fine."

She swallowed, her voice low and strained. "You don't understand. If they find us… if they find *me* with you… it would mean everything I've worked for is over. I'd be branded a traitor."

He reached out, his hand resting gently on her shoulder. "Lyra, we don't have to stay here if it's too dangerous for you. I can go ahead."

The suggestion struck her like a blow, her instincts warring with her emotions. The easy answer, the safe answer, would be to let him go, to watch him disappear into the forest and return to her clan with no one the wiser. But as she looked at him, a new fear gripped her—one she hadn't expected. The thought of losing him, of letting him go so easily, filled her with a kind of dread she couldn't ignore.

She shook her head, her voice fierce. "No. I won't leave you."

"Are you sure?" he asked softly, his eyes searching hers. "You've spent your whole life proving yourself to them. I don't want to be the reason that's taken from you."

Her jaw tightened, her gaze flickering back to the shadows where her clan's patrol passed. "And maybe that's the problem. Maybe proving myself means more than just following their rules. Maybe it's about… about finding my own way."

Kian's face softened, a glimmer of pride in his expression. "Then stay with me, Lyra. But only if that's what *you* want."

She looked down, her fingers twisting in the fabric of her tunic as her heart pounded. Her whole life had been defined by her clan's expectations, by the rigid discipline and loyalty they demanded. She'd never questioned it, never doubted that her path was laid out for her, clear and unyielding. But now, hiding in the shadows with Kian, the very rules she'd followed so diligently felt suffocating.

As the patrol's voices faded, Lyra let out a shaky breath, the tension in her body easing, though her heart remained conflicted. The fear of discovery had been real, visceral, but it had also illuminated something she couldn't ignore. The fear wasn't just about being caught; it was about what she would be willing to do if her clan forced her to choose between them and the person she was becoming.

After a long silence, she looked up at Kian, her voice steady but tinged with vulnerability. "I don't know if I'm ready to abandon everything. But… I don't think I can go back to who I was either."

He smiled, his gaze filled with quiet understanding. "Then don't. Keep going forward, step by step. You don't have to make every decision right now. Just… stay true to what feels right for you."

She nodded, her resolve growing, even as uncertainty lingered. Hiding here, in the quiet of the forest with Kian, she felt a sense of freedom she hadn't known she was missing. For the first time, the pull between loyalty to her clan and loyalty to herself didn't feel like a battle—it felt like the beginning of a new path.

They remained in the shadows a little while longer, Lyra's heart slowly settling as she let herself accept the choice she had already begun to make, piece by piece. And as they moved deeper into the forest, she knew that whatever lay ahead, she would face it as herself, not just as a loyal warrior, but as a woman ready to follow her own truth.

As they continued deeper into the forest, the silence between them was heavy, laden with unspoken words. Lyra felt Kian's presence beside her, steady and warm, a quiet assurance that had come to mean more to her than she'd ever anticipated. But with every step, her mind churned, torn between the loyalty ingrained in her and the undeniable pull of something new, something… freeing.

Kian glanced at her, his expression thoughtful. "Lyra," he began, his voice soft, "we don't have to keep walking this same path. We could leave the forest together. Start over. Just you and me."

She stopped, his words striking her like a jolt. "Leave?" she whispered, her eyes wide. "Kian, I… I can't just walk away."

"Can't you?" he replied gently, his gaze unwavering. "What's really holding you back? Is it your clan's expectations, or your own fear of breaking free?"

Lyra looked down, her throat tightening. "It's not that simple. My clan… they've given me everything. Discipline, purpose. Without them, I don't know who I am."

Kian took a step closer, his voice a mixture of warmth and determination. "But you're more than just their soldier, Lyra. You're someone who's brave enough to question, to care, to want something beyond duty. Don't you think that matters?"

Her hands shook as she clutched the edge of her cloak. "It's not that I don't want to go with you. I just… I don't know if I can live with the idea of abandoning my clan. They need me."

"Maybe," he said quietly, his voice soft but steady. "But what about what *you* need?"

She looked at him, her heart pounding. "I don't know what that is. For so long, I've only known one way of life. I don't even know where I'd begin if I… if I chose to leave."

Kian reached out, his hand warm as it brushed against hers. "You'd begin with me. We could go somewhere new, somewhere free of rules and expectations. A place where you're not bound by anyone else's vision of who you should be."

She felt her heart swell, the image he painted so vivid, so tempting. "And what if I'm not strong enough to let go? What if I regret it?"

He smiled, a gentle understanding in his eyes. "Then we face that together. Life is full of risks, Lyra. But sometimes, the risk is worth it. Sometimes, stepping into the unknown is the only way to find yourself."

Her voice was barely more than a whisper. "You really believe that?"

"Yes," he said, his tone unwavering. "I believe in you. I believe that you're more than what they've made you. And I believe that you have the strength to choose your own path, even if it's not the one they would choose for you."

Lyra swallowed, her gaze dropping as a surge of emotion swept over her. "But if I go with you… if I leave… I'm afraid of what that says about me. About my loyalty."

Kian's grip on her hand tightened, his eyes full of quiet resolve. "Loyalty isn't about giving up who you are. It's about honoring your truth. And maybe, just maybe, staying true to yourself is the highest form of loyalty there is."

She looked up, meeting his gaze, her defenses slipping further. "I want to believe that. I want to believe that I could be more, that there's something beyond the life I've always known."

"Then let yourself believe it," he urged softly. "Let yourself see what life could be like without the walls, without the weight of expectations."

For a long, heart-pounding moment, she allowed herself to imagine it—leaving the forest beside him, stepping into a new life with no rules, no demands. A life where she was free to be herself, to discover who she was without the constant pull of duty. She felt a surge of emotion, a deep longing she hadn't known existed, rising within her.

But then the reality set in, the teachings of her clan echoing in her mind, reminding her of the commitment she'd made, the loyalty that had defined her entire life. Her heart sank, and she pulled her hand away, her voice trembling. "I… I can't. Not yet. My duty—it's still a part of me. It's all I've ever known."

Kian's expression softened, and though disappointment flickered in his eyes, he nodded with understanding. "I understand, Lyra. This is your choice, and I would never try to take that from you."

She looked away, fighting the sting of tears. "Thank you for... for offering me this. For helping me see that there could be something else."

"You deserve to see that," he said quietly. "And whether or not you ever choose to take it, know that I'm here. I'll be here for as long as you need."

She forced herself to nod, the weight of her decision settling heavily over her. "Maybe one day I'll be ready to let go. To follow my own path."

He smiled, a warmth in his eyes that eased the ache in her chest. "Then I'll be waiting, Lyra. Whenever you're ready."

They stood in silence for a moment, the forest quiet around them. And though she hadn't chosen freedom, hadn't yet taken that leap into the unknown, a small part of her knew that, with Kian by her side, the possibility was there. It was something she could return to, a path she could still take, if ever she found the strength.

For now, though, she would continue forward, carrying the weight of her loyalty and her longing, hoping that, one day, the choice would feel a little less impossible.

Chapter 14
The Weight of Loyalty

They stood at the edge of the forest, where the dense trees thinned out, giving way to open land under a wide sky. Lyra and Kian had walked in silence, both knowing that the end of their journey together was near. The quiet between them was heavier than any words, thick with the weight of all the unspoken truths Lyra could feel pressing against her heart.

Kian turned to her, his expression calm but touched with sadness. "So, this is it," he said, his voice soft. "Back to the life we each came from."

Lyra looked down, her fingers fidgeting with the edge of her cloak. She couldn't meet his gaze; the thought of parting felt too raw, too final. "It feels strange," she murmured, barely able to keep the tremor from her voice. "To think of going back to how things were. After... everything."

Kian nodded, a faint smile tugging at his lips. "You're not the same person who walked into this forest, Lyra. And neither am I. It's not something you can forget."

She glanced up at him, her chest tightening. "I'm not sure what I am anymore. You've... changed things for me. Made me question things I never thought I'd question."

His gaze softened, a flicker of hope in his eyes. "Maybe that's not such a bad thing. Sometimes, questioning is the only way to find answers we didn't know we needed."

Lyra's throat tightened, the conflict within her bubbling to the surface. "I know. But it's not that simple. Returning to my clan means... letting go of all of this. Going back to their expectations, to the person I was trained to be."

"And is that what you want?" Kian asked quietly, his gaze unwavering. "To go back and pretend none of this ever happened?"

She looked away, her voice a whisper. "I don't know. I don't know if I have a choice. My clan has rules, expectations. They wouldn't understand... they'd never accept what I feel now."

He took a step closer, his hand hovering near hers. "But what do you feel, Lyra? What does *your* heart want?"

Her heart pounded, his question reverberating through her like a challenge. She closed her eyes, trying to hold back the surge of emotion. "It wants... it wants more than what my clan has taught me. But I don't know if that's allowed. I don't know if I have the right to want anything beyond duty."

Kian's voice was gentle but filled with conviction. "You do. You have every right to feel, to want, to live beyond the rules they set for you. That's your choice, not theirs."

She swallowed, her voice thick. "And what if they see that as betrayal? I can't just abandon them."

"You're not abandoning anyone by choosing yourself, Lyra," he replied softly. "Maybe it's just another way of showing them who you really are. Of being true to yourself."

She looked up, meeting his gaze, the pain and longing in her eyes clear. "You make it sound so simple. But for me, it's not. I can't just walk away."

He reached out, his hand gently brushing her cheek, his touch warm and grounding. "I'm not asking you to walk away. I'm just asking you to remember that you have the power to choose. And that maybe, one day, you'll choose a path that feels right for you."

Her chest tightened, her voice barely a whisper. "And what if that path leads me away from you?"

Kian smiled, a mixture of sadness and acceptance in his eyes. "Then I'll know that you're following your truth. That's all I could ever want for you."

They stood in silence, the weight of the moment pressing down on them. Lyra felt her resolve weakening, the ache of parting from him stirring a depth of emotion she hadn't allowed herself to feel. She wanted to tell him everything—how his presence had changed her, how he'd shown her a glimpse of a life beyond duty, one that felt both terrifying and beautiful.

But the words stuck in her throat, and all she could manage was, "I don't know how to say goodbye to you."

He gave her a soft, sad smile. "Then don't. Just say, 'See you again,' because even if we part here, a part of you will stay with me. And a part of me, with you."

A tear slipped down her cheek, and she quickly wiped it away, forcing a shaky smile. "Then… see you again, Kian. And thank you. For everything."

He nodded, his gaze lingering on her. "See you again, Lyra. Remember what you've seen here, what you've felt. And if you ever need to find your way back… I'll be waiting."

With one last look, Kian turned and began walking away, his figure slowly disappearing into the shadows of the trees. Lyra watched him go, a thousand unspoken words and feelings swirling within her, leaving her both hollow and full.

And as she stood there, alone once more, she knew that her life could never be the same. Whatever path she chose, whether for duty or for herself, Kian's presence would remain, a reminder of the freedom she had tasted, of the courage she had glimpsed within herself.

Slowly, she turned back toward her clan's path, her heart heavy yet filled with a newfound resolve. For now, she would return. But deep down, she knew this was only the beginning of a journey—one she was finally ready to take, with Kian's words echoing in her heart: that she had the power to choose.

As Lyra walked through the forest, her mind lingered on her final moments with Kian, his words echoing softly, resonating with truths she hadn't been ready to face. The path back to her clan was familiar, worn into the forest floor by years of disciplined footsteps. But now, it felt foreign, each step heavier, as though the trees themselves were asking her to pause, to reconsider.

A memory surfaced, vivid and sharp: Mirror Lake, where she'd confronted a reflection of herself she hadn't recognized. It felt like a lifetime ago, yet the memory stirred something within her, a reminder of the truth she had glimpsed beneath her carefully maintained facade.

In that moment at the lake, she'd seen herself as someone different—someone with a softer expression, a freer stance, a woman unburdened by the weight of her clan's rigid expectations. That reflection had haunted her, offering a glimpse of a life she hadn't allowed herself to imagine. But now, the memory filled her with a quiet determination, an understanding that perhaps that version of herself was not so distant, not so unattainable.

The Lyra she had seen in Mirror Lake had been unguarded, her eyes holding a lightness she'd never seen in her own reflection before. She'd felt unnerved then, but now, that image seemed to offer comfort. That version of herself wasn't bound by duty alone; she was someone who could choose, who could feel deeply, and who wasn't afraid of what those feelings might mean.

Her mind replayed Kian's words once more: *You have the power to choose. To follow a path that feels right for you.*

She paused, her gaze drifting to the dense forest around her, where dappled sunlight filtered through the branches. Standing there, she allowed herself to feel the pull of both paths—the one leading back to her clan, heavy with tradition and expectation, and the path she could barely see, one shrouded in uncertainty but glimmering with possibility.

The clan's rules had provided structure, but they had also created boundaries that restricted who she could be. She thought of her training, the endless drills that had shaped her, hardened her into a disciplined warrior. And yet, at Mirror Lake, she had seen another side to herself, a side that wasn't defined by loyalty or duty alone but by the quiet, undeniable desire for something more.

Lyra took a steadying breath, her heart thrumming with a newfound resolve. She didn't know what the future held, didn't know if she could ever fully embrace that reflection she'd seen. But she understood now that to honor her true self, she had to try.

The image of herself at Mirror Lake, of the freer, lighter woman she had glimpsed, lingered in her mind. That woman had felt joy, had known the relief of letting go, if only for a moment. That version of herself felt like a whisper of hope, a reminder that change wasn't something to be feared—it was something to reach for, something to embrace.

Slowly, Lyra resumed walking, the memory of Mirror Lake strengthening her steps. She didn't have all the answers yet, but she knew that her journey would no longer be confined to the path others had set for her. For the first time, she felt ready to carve her own way, a path that honored both her loyalty and her own heart.

And as she moved forward, her heart lifted, the weight of her doubts lightened by the knowledge that, somewhere along the way, she would find the balance she sought. She would honor her clan, but she would honor herself, too—no matter how long it took, no matter where it led.

Lyra had thought the parting was behind her, that the decision to return to her clan had been made. But as she reached the clearing, Kian was there, waiting, his figure illuminated by the soft glow of twilight. She stopped, her heart racing as she took in his steady gaze, the warmth in his eyes. He had come back, just as she was trying to leave.

"Kian," she murmured, the name catching in her throat, a blend of surprise and emotion she hadn't anticipated.

He stepped forward, his expression intense yet calm. "Lyra… I couldn't leave without saying this."

She swallowed, bracing herself, but the intensity of his gaze unsettled her. "Kian, you don't have to—"

"I do," he interrupted gently, his voice unwavering. "You have to know how I feel."

Her breath hitched as he continued, his words unguarded and sincere.

"These days with you, Lyra… I've felt something I didn't think I'd find. I see your strength, your loyalty, your heart. And somehow, you've become a part of me," he admitted, his voice softening as he searched her eyes. "I don't want to imagine my life without you in it."

Lyra's heart pounded as she took in his words, each one stirring the emotions she'd tried so hard to contain. She wanted to respond, to tell him how much he'd changed her, but a heavy dread held her back—the reminder of her clan's rules, the loyalty they demanded. Yet, standing here with him, that loyalty felt like both a shield and a burden.

"Kian, I… I don't know what to say," she whispered, her voice trembling.

"Then just say the truth, Lyra," he replied softly, his gaze unwavering. "I'm not asking you to choose between me and your clan. I just want to know where your heart stands."

She closed her eyes, struggling to gather her thoughts, but the conflicting emotions were overwhelming. "My heart is… torn," she admitted, her voice barely above a whisper. "I don't want to betray my clan. They're my family, my purpose. But with you… I feel like I can finally be myself."

His expression softened, understanding in his eyes. "And maybe that's the real choice here, Lyra. Not choosing between me or your clan, but choosing to be true to yourself."

Her gaze dropped, the weight of his words settling heavily on her. "But what if being true to myself means breaking the rules, going against everything I was taught?"

"Then maybe those rules were never meant to define you completely," he said, his voice filled with quiet conviction. "You're more than just a soldier, Lyra. You're a person with her own heart, her own desires."

She met his gaze, her voice filled with uncertainty. "And what if I choose to follow my heart, but lose everything else in the process? What if this path leads me away from everything I've ever known?"

Kian's hand reached for hers, his touch gentle but grounding. "Then at least you'll know that you chose for yourself. And that, Lyra, is something no one can take from you."

Her breath caught, the truth of his words piercing through the fear and uncertainty. She felt drawn to him, closer than she had ever let herself be with anyone. Yet, the fear of letting go, of crossing that line and abandoning everything familiar, loomed large.

"You don't know what you're asking of me," she whispered, her voice barely holding steady.

He smiled, a warmth in his eyes that eased her hesitation. "I know it's a lot. But I also know that if you don't let yourself feel this, you'll never know what could be. And I think… I think you owe it to yourself to find out."

Lyra's gaze lingered on his, the wall she'd built around her heart crumbling piece by piece. "You really believe that I can be both? Loyal to my clan and true to myself?"

He nodded, his voice filled with quiet certainty. "I do. Because the Lyra I see—the one who questions, who feels, who cares—that's someone who can create her own path, even if it's different from what was expected."

A long silence stretched between them, the weight of her choice hanging in the air. She felt the pull between duty and desire, between loyalty and freedom, more keenly than ever. Her heart ached, the fear and longing mingling in a way she'd never experienced before. But Kian's words, his presence, made her want to try—to see if there was a way to bridge the gap between the life she'd always known and the one she yearned for.

Finally, she took a shaky breath, her voice soft but resolute. "I don't know what the future holds, Kian. I don't know if I can balance this, or if it will end the way we want."

He smiled, his hand still holding hers. "That's all right. The future doesn't have to be certain. I'm just asking for a chance to see where this can lead."

She squeezed his hand, a hint of a smile tugging at her lips. "Then… maybe I can give it a chance. For now."

He chuckled softly, relief evident in his eyes. "That's all I ask, Lyra. One step at a time."

They stood in silence, the twilight settling around them like a quiet promise. And though the uncertainty remained, Lyra felt a surge of hope, a quiet thrill at the thought of exploring this new path, however unknown. For the first time, she was ready to take a risk—not just for him, but for herself.

The quiet between them was filled with an unspoken tension as the last traces of twilight melted into the night. Lyra felt the weight of Kian's presence beside her, a warmth that had once been unfamiliar but now felt like home. She wanted to hold onto this moment, to freeze time so she wouldn't have to face the inevitable decision, but reality pressed in, demanding she confront it.

Kian broke the silence, his voice gentle but steady. "Lyra… we both know where we're headed. I can't ask you to choose a path you're not ready for."

She looked down, her fingers tracing the hem of her cloak as she wrestled with her emotions. "I know," she whispered. "But that doesn't make it any easier."

He nodded, understanding in his gaze. "I never thought it would be. I knew, from the beginning, that the choice would be yours, no matter what I wanted."

Lyra swallowed, her throat tight. "And what do you want, Kian?"

He paused, his eyes softening as he looked at her. "I want you to be free. Free to make your own choices, to find your own way. Even if that path leads away from me."

She closed her eyes, the ache in her chest intensifying. "You say that as if it's easy, as if leaving you behind is something I can just... do."

He stepped closer, his hand reaching out to gently cup her shoulder. "I don't expect it to be easy. But I want you to know that whatever you decide, I understand. I'll respect it, even if it means we go our separate ways."

A shiver ran through her, the thought of parting feeling like an open wound she couldn't heal. She'd faced countless challenges, had been trained to withstand pain, but this was different. The idea of moving forward without him, of returning to her clan as if nothing had changed, felt almost impossible.

"Is it wrong," she murmured, her voice trembling, "that I want both? To honor my duty but... but still keep a part of this? Of you?"

Kian's gaze softened, a quiet sadness in his eyes. "No, Lyra. It's not wrong. It's human. But sometimes, life doesn't allow us to have both. Sometimes we have to let go to be true to ourselves."

Her heart twisted, a part of her wanting to argue, to insist there must be a way to balance both worlds. But deep down, she knew he was right. She couldn't hold onto everything without risking the very loyalty that had shaped her life. And yet, the thought of losing him left her feeling hollow.

Taking a deep breath, she forced herself to meet his gaze. "So… we part ways?"

He nodded, his voice barely more than a whisper. "For now. But that doesn't mean it's the end. Maybe one day, our paths will cross again, when we're both ready."

She wanted to believe him, to cling to that hope, but a part of her knew that her clan's expectations would never allow her the freedom to pursue something so uncertain, so personal. Still, she gave him a faint, bittersweet smile. "Maybe. Maybe one day."

They stood in silence, the enormity of the moment settling over them, both aware that this was more than a simple farewell. It was a choice, a decision that would define their lives in ways they couldn't yet understand.

Kian took her hand, his touch warm and grounding. "Whatever happens, Lyra, know that you changed me. You showed me what strength really looks like. And that… that will always stay with me."

She squeezed his hand, her voice choked with emotion. "And you showed me what it means to feel free, even if only for a moment. I'll carry that with me."

He released her hand slowly, reluctance evident in his gaze, but he stepped back, giving her space to make her choice without pressure. She watched him, her heart torn between two worlds—the disciplined, loyal warrior her clan expected her to be and the woman who had found something beautiful and terrifying in his presence.

Finally, she turned away, each step heavy with the weight of her decision. She knew that going back to her clan meant leaving behind the possibilities she'd glimpsed with Kian, but it was a sacrifice she felt bound to make. Yet, as she walked, she couldn't shake the feeling that a part of her heart remained behind, rooted to this place, tied to him.

And as the forest swallowed her once more, Lyra knew that this choice would linger, echoing in her heart—a reminder that, while she might be loyal to her clan, a piece of herself would forever belong to the one who had shown her the meaning of freedom.

Chapter 15
The Heart's Awakening

Lyra stepped through the stone archway that marked the boundary of her clan's village, her footsteps heavy, her heart weighed down by an unfamiliar sense of distance. The village was exactly as she'd left it—the rhythmic clang of metal from the forge, the voices of children laughing, the disciplined footsteps of her fellow warriors as they sparred in the training yard. Every sight and sound was the same, yet now it felt foreign, as if she were seeing it through someone else's eyes.

As she walked, a few of her clanmates greeted her, nodding with respectful recognition. "Welcome back, Lyra," one of the older warriors called out, his eyes showing approval. "You did well. The council has spoken highly of your commitment."

She managed a faint smile, her response automatic. "Thank you, Orrin. It's... good to be back."

But the words felt hollow, empty. She glanced around, the familiarity of her surroundings only amplifying the disconnection she felt. Every person she passed, every structure she saw, reminded her of the duty she had upheld for so long, of the life she'd once embraced without question. But now, a deeper understanding gnawed at her, a sense of something missing that she couldn't ignore.

As she made her way toward the main hall, Kara, her closest friend since childhood, approached her with a grin. "There you are! We were starting to think the forest had swallowed you whole."

Lyra forced a laugh, though it felt strained. "The forest almost did… in more ways than one."

Kara's smile faded, replaced by concern. "Lyra, are you all right? You don't look like yourself."

She hesitated, the urge to confide in Kara rising within her. But how could she explain what she was feeling? How could she describe the transformation that had taken place within her, the bond she had formed with Kian, the freedom she had glimpsed?

"I'm fine," she replied, her tone clipped. "It was just… an intense journey."

Kara narrowed her eyes, clearly unconvinced. "Are you sure? You've been through the forest a hundred times before, and you've never looked so… unsettled."

Lyra glanced down, swallowing the truth she couldn't voice. "Things were different this time."

"Different how?" Kara pressed, her voice softer, her concern genuine.

Lyra hesitated, feeling the words pressing against her throat, desperate to escape. "I… I saw things in myself I hadn't seen before. Felt things I wasn't prepared for."

Kara's brows knitted together in confusion. "Things like what? Doubt?"

"Maybe," Lyra said, her voice barely more than a whisper. "Doubt, yes, but also… questions about everything. About who I am, what I truly want. About whether the life I've been living is… enough."

Kara's eyes softened, but her tone grew more serious. "Lyra, we're warriors. This is our purpose. Your duty is who you are. We all have moments of doubt, but that's all they are—moments. They pass."

Lyra looked away, the words hollow in her ears. "Maybe. Or maybe there's more to it."

Kara's voice dropped to a whisper, a hint of alarm creeping into her tone. "Lyra, you sound like… like someone who's questioning her loyalty."

The words struck Lyra like a blow, and she stiffened, the familiar instinct to defend herself rising. "No," she said quickly, a flicker of fear in her eyes. "I would never betray my loyalty."

But even as she spoke, the weight of her words hung heavily in the air, laced with an uncertainty she couldn't mask. She knew that, in her heart, she had begun to question everything—her place in the clan, her role as a warrior, the loyalty that had once defined her. The forest, her time with Kian, the reflections she'd seen… they had all opened a door within her, one she didn't know how to close.

Kara's gaze softened, though the concern in her eyes remained. "Lyra, I don't know what happened out there, but whatever it was… maybe you need to talk to the council. They can help you find clarity, remind you of who you are."

Lyra shook her head, the idea of the council filling her with a sense of dread. "I don't think the council can help with this, Kara. This is… something I have to figure out on my own."

A flicker of sadness crossed Kara's face, and she reached out, placing a hand on Lyra's shoulder. "Just remember, whatever you're feeling, you're not alone. We're your family, Lyra. And whatever doubts you have, we're here to keep you grounded."

Lyra managed a tight smile, her heart aching with the conflict swirling inside her. "Thank you, Kara. That means a lot."

But as she watched her friend walk away, the familiar sights and sounds of her clan closing in around her, she felt the dissonance deepen, the divide between who she had been and who she was becoming growing more distinct. Her experience in the forest had changed her irreversibly, and she could no longer ignore the questions that had taken root within her heart.

Standing there, surrounded by her people, Lyra realized that she was still a stranger in the place she had once called home. And the only thing she was certain of was that the answers she sought wouldn't be found within the walls of her clan—they lay somewhere beyond, waiting for her to find them.

Lyra sat alone in the small, dimly lit room that had been her sanctuary since her earliest training days. Outside, she could hear the faint hum of her clan's nightly routines—the clash of sparring weapons, the low murmurs of warriors discussing strategy, the footsteps of those dedicated to maintaining order and discipline. But for the first time, those sounds felt distant, muffled by the whirlwind of thoughts that swirled in her mind.

Her gaze drifted to the window, where the sky was a dark indigo, speckled with stars. She remembered a night not unlike this one, standing under a similar sky in the heart of the forest, side by side with Kian. The memory was sharp, vivid, as if he were there beside her again, his presence filling the room with an undeniable warmth. She could almost hear his voice, that calm, steady tone that always seemed to cut through her defenses.

"Lyra," he had said that night, his eyes reflecting the starlight, "you're allowed to want more than just duty. You're allowed to feel, to be free."

She closed her eyes, the weight of his words pressing down on her. In that moment, she had felt a spark of hope, a glimmer of a life where she wasn't bound by her clan's expectations, where she could choose her own path, even if it was uncertain. But now, back within the walls of her clan, that spark felt like a distant memory, slipping through her fingers like sand.

A knock at her door pulled her from her thoughts. It was Orrin, his face shadowed with concern. "Lyra, may I come in?"

She nodded, gesturing for him to enter. He closed the door quietly, settling into the chair across from her. "Word around the camp is that something's troubling you," he said gently, his tone probing yet kind. "You've always been one of the strongest, most loyal among us. But I see hesitation in your eyes. What happened out there, Lyra?"

She hesitated, the words catching in her throat. "I… met someone," she admitted softly, her gaze fixed on the floor. "He showed me things—about myself, about what life could be. Things I never thought possible."

Orrin's brow furrowed, his expression a mix of curiosity and concern. "Someone outside the clan?"

She nodded, her voice barely more than a whisper. "Yes. His name is Kian. He made me question… everything."

Orrin let out a slow breath, the worry in his eyes deepening. "And what did he make you question?"

"My loyalty," she said, her voice breaking slightly. "For so long, I believed that my duty was everything, that my purpose was to serve without question. But now… now I don't know if that's true. I don't know if it's enough."

Orrin leaned forward, his gaze intent. "Lyra, loyalty is the foundation of who we are. Without it, we're lost. Whatever this Kian has told you, don't let it cloud your purpose. You are a warrior, bound to this clan. We are your family."

She looked away, her voice trembling. "But what if there's more to life than duty? What if there's a part of me that longs for freedom, for a life beyond these walls?"

Orrin's expression hardened, his voice firm. "Freedom is a luxury, Lyra. It's not what makes us strong. Strength is found in discipline, in sacrifice. You know this. We all do."

She felt her throat tighten, her mind echoing with Kian's words. *You're more than just their soldier. You have the right to choose your own path.*

But Orrin's voice brought her back to reality, grounding her. "Whatever you felt with this outsider, it's temporary. A distraction. When you chose this life, you committed yourself to a higher purpose. That doesn't change because of fleeting desires."

"Maybe it wasn't fleeting," she murmured, barely daring to meet his gaze. "Maybe it was real. Maybe it's a part of me I can't ignore anymore."

Orrin shook his head, his voice sharp. "Lyra, you're speaking of defiance. Betrayal. Are you really willing to turn your back on everything we've taught you, everything we stand for?"

She flinched, the weight of his words settling heavily in her chest. "No," she whispered, though the doubt lingered. "I don't want to betray anyone. I just… I want to understand who I am, beyond the rules."

Orrin's face softened, his voice lowering. "Then remember that who you are is someone dedicated to this clan. Someone who has given her life to protect and serve. Don't let a stranger's influence make you forget that."

She nodded slowly, the truth of his words mingling with the pull of her memories with Kian. The loyalty she felt for her clan was real, a part of her she couldn't erase. But now, she was beginning to see that loyalty didn't have to come at the expense of her own heart, her own choices.

After a moment, Orrin rose to his feet, placing a hand on her shoulder. "You're strong, Lyra. Stronger than any doubt. Don't let yourself waver."

She forced a small, tight smile, watching him leave. But as the door closed behind him, she felt more conflicted than ever. She couldn't ignore the yearning within her, the desire for freedom that Kian had awakened. And yet, the loyalty she felt for her clan was deeply rooted, woven into her very being.

Sitting alone, she realized that the choice was no longer just between loyalty and freedom. It was a choice to define her own strength, to reconcile her duty with the quiet hope that perhaps, someday, she could embrace both without having to abandon either.

The next morning, Lyra was summoned to the council hall. The summons had been delivered with the quiet urgency that signaled something more than a routine debriefing. As she walked through the village toward the hall, her heart beat heavily, her mind replaying her conversation with Orrin. She knew her clan well enough to sense that her inner turmoil hadn't gone unnoticed, that her questions and doubts had left a mark that no amount of discipline could disguise.

Inside the hall, the air was tense, thick with the authority of the clan's council members, who sat in a semicircle at the front of the room. Each face was familiar, yet now they seemed to watch her with a quiet, intense scrutiny. At the center of the semicircle was Elder Ren, her clan's chief leader, whose gaze was as unyielding as steel.

"Lyra," he began, his voice deep and measured. "We have heard rumors, whispers of... changes within you. Your time in the forest seems to have left its mark."

She straightened, forcing herself to remain calm, her voice steady. "I don't understand, Elder Ren. I've always served loyally."

Ren's eyes narrowed, and he exchanged a glance with Elder Mora, who sat beside him. Mora's expression was grave, her tone sharper than Ren's. "Loyalty is not just about serving, Lyra. It's about embodying the values of our clan, living them without question. We sense a shift in you, a hesitation that was not there before."

Lyra felt the weight of their scrutiny pressing down on her, and her mind flashed with memories of Kian's words, his insistence that she had a choice, that she could be more than just their soldier. She struggled to keep her composure, but the council's unwavering gaze felt like it was peeling away the layers she'd tried so hard to protect.

"I have done my duty," she replied, her voice firmer than she felt. "Whatever doubts you think you see… they do not affect my loyalty."

Ren's gaze remained steady, but there was an edge to his voice. "Do you truly believe that? We are not blind, Lyra. We know that you encountered someone in the forest. Someone who has… influenced you."

Lyra's heart skipped a beat, but she forced herself to hold his gaze. "Yes. I met someone. But that does not mean my loyalty has changed."

Mora leaned forward, her expression unrelenting. "And yet, you hesitate. Your loyalty to this clan should be beyond question, yet here you stand, struggling to answer us directly."

Lyra felt a surge of frustration, the careful walls she'd built beginning to crack. "Perhaps I hesitate because… because I am realizing that loyalty doesn't mean abandoning my own heart."

The words slipped out before she could stop them, and the silence that followed was palpable, each council member's gaze sharpening. Elder Ren's expression darkened, his voice low and warning. "Loyalty, Lyra, is not something to mold to one's desires. It is an absolute. To question it is to betray it."

Her jaw clenched, the internal conflict rising to the surface, the weight of her feelings pushing back against the rigid expectations of her clan. "And what if I am more than just a warrior? What if there's a part of me that cannot be silenced by duty alone?"

Mora's eyes narrowed, her tone cold. "Then that part of you is dangerous, Lyra. That part of you must be eradicated if you are to remain among us. We cannot have a warrior whose loyalty wavers, whose mind is clouded by outside influences."

Lyra's pulse quickened, her heart pounding in her chest as she felt the divide between herself and the council widening. The quiet hope she'd carried since her time with Kian, the glimmer of a life beyond duty, began to flare within her, challenging the unwavering discipline she'd always known.

"I cannot deny what I've seen, what I've felt," she said, her voice steadying, her courage building despite the council's disapproval. "I cannot be only what the clan expects if it means losing a part of myself."

Ren's face hardened, his voice sharp with finality. "Then you must choose, Lyra. Either you banish this foolishness and return to the life of a true warrior, or you accept that this clan will no longer accept you as one of its own."

Lyra felt the weight of his words settle over her like a stone, the truth she'd avoided confronting now glaringly clear. There was no longer any hiding, no longer any pretense. She had to decide—either to suppress the part of herself that Kian had awakened, the part that yearned for freedom, or to step into a future unknown, one that would separate her from the life she had always known.

She drew in a deep breath, her voice steady as she met Elder Ren's gaze. "I understand, Elder Ren. I have always honored my duty. But perhaps loyalty, true loyalty, is about being honest with oneself."

A murmur rippled through the council members, shock and disapproval mingling in their expressions. Ren's gaze remained cold, unmoved. "Then it seems you have already made your choice, Lyra. Consider carefully, for once this path is taken, there is no returning."

She held his gaze, a quiet resolve settling within her. The fear, the uncertainty, all remained, but beneath it was a strength she hadn't known she possessed. "I understand."

With that, she turned and left the hall, her heart pounding, her mind racing with the enormity of what she'd done. She knew she was leaving behind more than just a role—she was leaving behind a way of life, a part of herself that had been forged through years of discipline and sacrifice. But as she stepped out into the open air, the pull of freedom, of being true to herself, was undeniable.

And though the future was uncertain, for the first time, Lyra felt she was ready to face it, not as a warrior bound by duty but as someone determined to discover her own path, wherever it might lead.

Lyra stepped outside the council hall, her heart racing as the gravity of her conversation with the elders settled over her. The village lay quiet in the late afternoon light, the familiar sounds and faces that had once been her anchor now felt distant, like echoes of a life that was slipping further from her grasp. She took a steadying breath, but before she could gather her thoughts, Orrin appeared beside her, his expression a mix of confusion and worry.

"Lyra," he said, his voice low but tense, "I heard… I heard what happened in there. Is it true? Are you really considering… leaving?"

Lyra met his gaze, the internal conflict surging within her once more. "Orrin, I… I don't know what I'm considering anymore. All I know is that I can't ignore the part of me that feels trapped."

He shook his head, his face etched with disbelief. "Trapped? Lyra, you're one of the best. You've been loyal your whole life. How can you even think of walking away from that?"

Her voice trembled, but she forced herself to speak, to put words to the feelings that had haunted her. "Because, Orrin, I'm starting to realize that maybe loyalty isn't just about following orders. Maybe it's about being true to yourself."

Orrin's eyes narrowed, his voice sharpening. "True to yourself? That's not what we were taught. The clan comes first, always. Without it, what do you have?"

Lyra took a deep breath, her voice steadier this time. "I have a part of me I've ignored for so long, I barely recognize it. And maybe… maybe it's time I stopped ignoring it."

A hint of anger flared in his eyes. "And what about the rest of us? Your friends? The people who trained with you, who trusted you? Are you ready to betray all of that because of some outsider's influence?"

"Kian didn't influence me," she replied, though her voice wavered. "He helped me see things I couldn't see on my own. Things I would have buried forever if I'd stayed here without question."

"So you're leaving," he said bitterly, crossing his arms. "After everything. Just like that?"

Her voice softened, the weight of his words settling over her. "It's not 'just like that,' Orrin. This is the hardest choice I've ever had to make. I'm giving up everything I've known, everyone I've cared about. But what I'm finding is… I can't give up myself."

Orrin's expression softened slightly, his voice lowering as he looked at her with a hint of sadness. "Lyra, we all have moments of doubt. But that doesn't mean we abandon our purpose. Our purpose is what defines us."

She shook her head slowly, a quiet resolve strengthening within her. "Maybe it used to define me. But now, I think purpose is something we choose. And I want to choose it for myself, not just accept it because it's what I was given."

They stood in silence for a long moment, the air thick with tension. Finally, Orrin sighed, a mixture of disappointment and resignation in his gaze. "So this is it, then? You're really going?"

Lyra looked down, the ache in her chest nearly unbearable. "I don't want to hurt you, or anyone else. But I have to find out who I am beyond these walls. I have to see if there's a place for me that I get to choose."

Orrin's jaw tightened, but he nodded slowly, his voice thick with emotion. "I don't agree with this, Lyra. But… I hope you find whatever it is you're looking for."

She offered him a faint, bittersweet smile. "Thank you, Orrin. That means more to me than you know."

He looked away, the pain in his eyes clear. "Just… don't forget where you came from. And know that there are people here who will remember you, even if you turn your back on us."

"I'll never forget," she whispered, the words laced with both sadness and conviction. "But this is something I have to do."

He nodded once, then turned and walked away, leaving her standing alone under the fading sunlight. She watched him go, her heart heavy, knowing that the bonds she'd held so dear were changing, that she was stepping away from the life she'd always known.

And as she turned toward the path that led beyond the village, Lyra felt a mixture of fear and exhilaration. For the first time, she was walking a path of her own choosing, with no orders, no obligations—only the quiet, thrilling possibility of freedom.

With a steadying breath, she took her first step forward, ready to embrace the unknown, her heart both shattered and whole, knowing that whatever lay ahead, it would be her journey, her life.

Epilogue
A Path of Her Own

The soft glow of dawn spread across the Forest of Reflections, casting long shadows that danced across the mist-covered ground. The air was cool, crisp, and the trees whispered as a gentle breeze stirred their leaves. Lyra stood at the edge of the forest, her gaze distant, reflecting on the choices that had brought her to this moment.

It had been months since she'd left her clan behind, since she'd walked away from everything she'd known. The decision had not come easily—she had wrestled with it, questioned herself a thousand times, but in the end, she couldn't ignore the pull of freedom, the undeniable truth that had been awakened in her heart. Kian's words had sparked something within her, something she hadn't been able to suppress, no matter how hard she tried.

Now, as she stood at the boundary between the forest and the unknown beyond, she felt the weight of that decision lifting from her shoulders. She had always been strong, disciplined, and loyal, but for the first time in her life, she felt free. Truly free.

A soft rustle behind her drew her attention, and she turned to see Kian approaching, his usual easy smile on his face. His presence was a comfort now, no longer an irritation. Over the past few months, they had grown closer, their partnership solidifying in ways she hadn't expected. Together, they had faced dangers, shared moments of quiet, and slowly but surely, she had let her guard down.

"Ready?" Kian asked, stopping beside her, his amber eyes glinting with amusement.

Lyra nodded, a faint smile tugging at the corners of her lips. "More than ready."

He studied her for a moment, his expression softening. "You know, when we first met, I didn't think you'd ever leave the clan. You seemed so… committed to that life."

"I was," Lyra admitted, her gaze drifting back to the horizon. "For a long time, I believed that duty was all that mattered. That loyalty to my clan defined who I was."

"And now?"

"Now I know that loyalty isn't about giving up who you are," she said, her voice quiet but firm. "It's about being true to yourself. And for me, that means choosing my own path."

Kian's smile widened, a hint of pride in his eyes. "I'm glad you figured that out. It looks good on you."

She rolled her eyes, but there was no malice in the gesture—only a fondness that had grown between them. "Don't get too cocky, Kian. I'm still figuring things out."

"Aren't we all?" he replied with a chuckle. "But hey, at least now you're doing it on your own terms."

Lyra nodded, the truth of his words sinking in. She had spent so much of her life bound by the expectations of others, by the rules and duties of her clan. But now, standing on the cusp of a new beginning, she felt the exhilarating rush of possibility. The world was vast, full of unknowns, and for the first time, she was ready to face it without fear.

They stood in comfortable silence for a moment, the sounds of the forest surrounding them. Lyra's mind drifted back to the countless nights she had spent patrolling these woods, always on alert, always vigilant. But now, the forest felt different—no longer a place of duty, but a place of reflection and growth. It had been in these woods that she had confronted her fears, her doubts, and ultimately, her true self.

"I think the forest was always trying to show me something," she said softly, more to herself than to Kian. "I just wasn't ready to see it."

Kian glanced at her, his expression thoughtful. "What do you think it was showing you?"

"That there's more to life than duty," she replied, her gaze far away. "That there's strength in letting go, in trusting yourself to find your own way."

He nodded, his eyes warm with understanding. "Sounds like you learned the lesson well."

They stood together for a few moments longer, the dawn spreading its golden light across the land. The future stretched out before them, wide and open, full of endless possibilities.

For the first time in her life, Lyra wasn't afraid of the unknown—she was ready to embrace it.

"Where to next?" Kian asked, his tone light but with a hint of curiosity.

Lyra smiled, the answer coming easily. "Wherever the wind takes us."

He grinned, his eyes shining with excitement. "I like the sound of that."

Together, they turned away from the forest, their footsteps light as they began to walk toward the horizon. The past was behind them now—her clan, her old life, the rules that had once bound her. Ahead of them lay a world of adventure, of freedom, and of choices she would make for herself.

And as they disappeared into the distance, Lyra felt the last of her doubts slip away, carried off by the breeze. She was no longer just a warrior, no longer defined by her loyalty to a single cause. She was Lyra—strong, free, and finally at peace with the path she had chosen.

The Forest of Reflections faded behind them, but its lessons would remain with her always. And as she stepped into the unknown, Lyra knew that whatever challenges lay ahead, she would face them with courage, with purpose, and with the knowledge that she was, at last, truly free.

In the heart of the Forest of Reflections, the trees whispered softly, their branches swaying in the breeze. The forest had seen many come and go, many who had sought answers, many who had faced their deepest fears. But few had left with the clarity that Lyra had found. And as the forest settled into its quiet rhythm once more, it seemed almost content, as though it had done its part in guiding her toward her true self.

Lyra would return one day, she knew that much. But when she did, it would not be as the same person who had once walked these woods in search of duty. She would return as someone who had discovered her own strength, her own purpose, and her own freedom. And the forest, in its infinite wisdom, would welcome her back with open arms.

For now, though, the world awaited. And Lyra was ready.